A GLORIOUS ARISING

A Journey to the Remembrance of Me

KIANA WEBB

A GLORIOUS ARISING:
A JOURNEY TO
THE REMEMBRANCE OF ME

ADVANCE PRAISE

I will forever be beyond amazed at how much a woman can persevere through trauma and pain. The many layers of complexity of how much she can carry, the weight and pressures in a world that's not too fond of the divine feminine energy that surely gives this world the balance it needs to avoid the total destruction of the human condition. None of us will get through this life without experiencing some tremendous heartache at some point along the way. Kiana Webb's memoir chronicles each life-altering event that contributed to the making of the woman whose words we read here in this honest telling of her story and all that she had to overcome to Rise to such a Glorious elevated vibration in time.

—Tony Rich
Grammy Award-winning Producer,
Singer Songwriter and Fine Artist

Kiana Webb's *A Glorious Arising* stands out as a beacon of objective truth and raw inspiration in the pantheon of memoirs that promise to break your heart and stitch it back together.

It's a rare gem that manages to be both smart and soulful, mixing wit with wisdom in a way that's as entertaining as it is enlightening. From the very beginning, Webb invites us into her world with the kind of charm and sincerity that feels like confiding in a lifelong friend over a cup of coffee.

At its core, *A Glorious Arising* is Webb's unflinching confrontation with her past, a journey from splintered innocence to a whole-hearted embrace of life. The memoir is cleverly structured in three parts, each marking a significant phase in Webb's path to self-discovery. It's not just a narrative; it's an odyssey that charts the tumultuous waters of early childhood trauma, the quest for self-love, and the pursuit of spiritual enlightenment.

She tackles topics like loneliness, self-esteem issues, and the pain of her early years with a blend of sharp insight and humor that never undermines the severity of her experiences. Instead, it makes her story more relatable and more human. Webb doesn't just recount events; she reflects on them, drawing readers into her internal dialogue with a brave and beautiful vulnerability.

In a deeply personal account of her journey to discover her best self, Webb lays bare her soul in a commitment to turning her narrative into a bridge for healing for others. The piece is a universal call to action for all of us to seek our own *Glorious Arising.* Smart, funny, and utterly charming, she brilliantly invites us to reconsider our own narratives, challenging us to find our inner light.

—Courtney Racquel Rhodes, Founder & Designer
Courtney Racquel Jewelry, and Co-Founder at C & D The Agency

The footsteps and the path taken to reveal her past without letting fear stop her truth led to Kiana's *A Glorious Arising.* Kiana Webb's book is a tour de force. With spirit soaring, and a mindset that laid the groundwork for her spiritual enlightenment of mind, body, and spirit, Kiana is a soldier of love who surrounds herself with kind spirits. Believers who are open to digging deeper into their inner beings will find, not only gems of insight but tools to help them along their way. Whatever stage of discovery you may be, believing in a positive state of mind, body, and spirit, allows God to steer your ship in a direction that helps you achieve what you have always desired. The sky is not the limit, you are.

—Anthony Liggins,
Abstract expressionist, creative director, author, Spiritual Warrior

In *A Glorious Arisings* Kiana Webb takes readers on a profound journey. Webb's spiritual awakening provides inspiration and practical tools for those seeking a similar journey a (*Glorious Arising*). This narrative of courage, love, and self-discovery serves as a beacon of inspiration for those seeking to embrace life, offering a deeply moving and empowering testament to the human spirit.

—Lucy Morillo, Esq.
Attorney and Serial Entrepreneur

Kiana Webb's book, *A Glorious Arising: A Journey To The Remembrance Of Me,* is more than a memoir; it's a map to reclaiming one's forgotten essence. Witness her courage and humility as she shares her story and navigates the path of spiritual awakening, shedding layers of fear, anxiety, and self-doubt to rediscover her magnificence within.

—Tammy Tumbling, President
Orange County Community Foundation

DEDICATION

For My Family
And to Everyone Who is Seeking Unconditional love.

I Love YOU!

TABLE OF CONTENTS

INTRODUCTION

☥

Meeting Kiana was a gift my soul needed. There are many lessons I took away from reading this book, and I am eternally grateful to her for being so vulnerable, honest, and above all, giving. Kiana is an example and the manifestation of one who has found the courage and humility to journey on a spiritual path to remember her soul's contract. Her gift to you, *A GLORIOUS ARISING: A JOURNEY TO THE REMEMBERANCE OF ME* is priceless.

Too many of us "living lives of quiet desperation," (Ralph Waldon Emmerson, *Walden*) are unaware we have the choice to unshackle from debilitating emotional conditions that disconnect us from ourselves.

Whatever the reason for disengaging from who you are at your core, fear, anxiety, anger, sadness—the discontent these misalignments produce, is a soul calling you to look inward. Imagine the life of one who early on identifies their sense of purpose. How much potential is inherent in such a life? How much more success could one have when living in harmony with oneself?

As one of the premises of this book suggests, doing life and doing you, is a choice. That message, however, can only be understood when the student is ready. Trusting the teacher will appear is the certainty spiritual acumen assures. But as Ralph Waldo Emerson said, "To be yourself in a world that is constantly trying to make you something else is the greatest accomplishment."

And that is hard work, especially in a world where mostly everyone is dressed to please. Learning to walk a new path requires courage and faith but the rewards of finding one's remembered self are transformative. I hope you honor the echoes of your heart and your soul.

Privileged to have journeyed with Kiana through her story, I am overjoyed to have been asked to write an introduction to this important work. I hope that anyone who is drawn to, and or inspired by this book, will come to appreciate that the difference between who you are, and who you want to be, lies in the choices you make and the lenses through which you view those choices. I hope you make good choices.

C. C. Avram
Author

PREFACE

☥

This might sound unbelievable, but I promise it's real. In my early forties, I had a surreal vision that felt like it came straight out of special effects in a movie. I was in my childhood home which I hadn't been to in over two decades. The familiar corridor was bathed in a bright, healing light, and bouncing off the hallway walls were rays in pink, yellow, and orange reminiscent of a scene where embraced by the light, people walk into Heaven.

Behind me, the door to my old bedroom stood ajar and in front of me, a pure, bright, white orb was spinning neon colors of the rainbow. The light evoked feelings of eternal love. Afraid of its vastness, the unknown, and of losing myself, I just stood there. Though desirous to walk through it, I was stuck. Halfway between my old and—current reality, I saw a little girl. The two of us are in the hallway together. We know each other. I look closely at the morphing figure and that little girl is me. Tears well in my eyes as I become aware of how grateful I am to her. So deeply grateful for all she had borne for me, I take her hand.

For too long I had been cut off from my emotions, compartmentalized, dissociated, and armored up, but this day I am beside her, feeling all the emotions she was not allowed to let surface. I want to thank her. I want to embrace her. I want to release her from all the pain and suffering she has stored in her being for so long and I want to let her know I got this from here on out. As we clasped hands, I finally sensed the missing link to my past I hadn't realized was not there—my integrated self.

In that moment of wholeness, I reconnected to all that I AM. Together, hand-in-hand, we walked toward the light. As we got closer, I looked at her and said, "It's okay, you can let go now. I will take care of us from now on." We merged into one and without hesitation moved into the light, disappearing into the beautiful essence of love. With certainty I then knew I was well on my way to being all I had ever imagined—a child of God. She and I, one and the same, despite the intergenerational trauma that kept us rooted in a place of silent suffering, were meant to fly. I was ready to be unstuck and to claim our greatness.

THE BACKSTORY

☥

I came into this world surrounded by love. That love however was based on expectation, judgment, and conditions, which often didn't feel anything like love. Many parents believe if they take care of the safety and security needs of their children, they are loving them unconditionally, not recognizing that a child's emotional and psychological needs are equally important. My childhood left me searching for years for who I AM. From a young age, in my bid to self-protect, I tried to fit in and be like everyone else. Then I tried to be like no one else, which left me lonely. Feelings of never being comfortable in my skin were some of the lessons I took away from my childhood experiences. It took Herculean effort and serious soul-searching for me to finally accept that pain, grief, sadness, aloneness, and hurt were steps along my way to claiming the life I desired. Unaware of the notion of a soul contract, it was only fair that I asked why my life had been so painful. Why had it thrown me into a cauldron? Or, why does a benevolent God allow people to suffer? What, too, I asked was the purpose of this grand experiment called human beings?

Regardless of culture, beliefs, upbringing, age, status, wealth, or popularity; the value or narrative about self and everyone/thing starts with you. How one reacts to perceptions; how they create behaviors and feelings that connect and disconnect them from divine love is always a choice to be made on the way to becoming.

Maybe like me, when you get to a point of seeing, feeling, and connecting to all of who you are, you will recognize everything, and I mean everything that happens in life, positive or negative, is for your good. No matter how "traumatic" your life may be or seem to have been; the power to unlock the doors standing between you and peace, joy, and self-love, is within—the divine existence of I AM. If you can believe everything happens in your life for your good, but that not everything feels good, you can begin to weave the life you desire. No matter the experience, it is designed to spur you on to choose unconditional love and to remember who you are at your essence—the remembrance of your soul.

The reality is, that if you're born into this world, chances are zero that you'll get a pass on experiencing pain and suffering. It is how you view and feel about those experiences that determine outcomes. I never really understood what it meant to love myself, and that's been my work; coming back to love. This is so big. It's bigger than all fears. It was bigger than my fears. Constantly going through this evolutionary process of acceptance of all of it, all of who I am, all of what was orchestrated to develop and make me into who I am, has been humbling. I am at a point where I recognize that without the things I experienced, I wouldn't have had the opportunity to be where I am right now. I can now stand alone as well as stand together, and it's a liberating feeling to love without fear and to know beyond a shadow of a doubt that love is what sets you free.

Everyone has a life story. How it is interpreted shapes our reality. Depending on how the narrative was impacted by love, it could evoke happy or sad feelings. Many of us experience both sides of the love equation. On our journey, if we encounter even just a smidgen of love from those guiding us, it feels like it makes the journey easier. For those whose journey back to self-love is devoid of any experience of love, it may feel like we need to work harder to find the love within. I wish I had known earlier, none of it is true. If you choose love, then it is already yours.

I have experienced both and have come to realize, no matter where I was, that everything that happened to me was moving me toward connectedness and I began to recognize and accept its purpose. If there is one thing to believe, it is that no matter how traumatic your life may be, the Universe has your back. This was not something I always felt.

My blind spot in finding a fulfilling life was in the feeling loved equation. To feel love and get acknowledgment the way I needed, meant I had to prove my value to be loved, so I created a life of being in service to my family sacrificing my own needs. Over time I began to resent them and the direction of my life. Feeling guilt and shame for resenting them, I tried harder to be of service. Shuttered in my cocoon of safety I was slipping further into depression. At the beginning of my spiritual journey, what I came to understand was I was in service to my family, but I wasn't in service to myself or God. What I was doing was simply manipulating the situation to get what I needed. At first I genuinely just wanted to help ease my mom and dad's burdens, but when that turned into accolades and recognition of my otherwise invisible self, I used it to seek love from them and then from everyone. The byproduct was service to my family, despite its origin, had proven to be a meaningful and necessary step along the way to finding *my* life. It had allowed me to see life from above and from below and that panoramic view prepared me for the kind of acceptance I have now found. It gave me a large swathe of choices and the push I needed.

If I am honest, I was completely disconnected from the goodness of life. Still, I instinctively made choices and somehow the Universe responded in ways that got me closer to the me I was meant to be. Twenty years ago, I found myself being called to sign my emails with *Faith, Hope,* and *Love.* They always seemed more meaningful than, *Sincerely, Respectfully, Best wishes* or *Always.* Little did I know it was portending the spiritual journey I would embark upon to find my true self.

Likewise, since grammar school I had been singing a song I often heard at church, *This Little Light of Mine, I'm Gonna Let it Shine.* I believed in that light but somehow could not find it in me. I kept looking for it because I had such an unexplained but profound longing—a restlessness in my spirit that never seemed to let me be. It wasn't until much later I understood that for my light to shine I had to wholeheartedly embrace the very words I had been closing all my correspondence with. I didn't need to just write them, I needed to live them. The teachings of Faith, Hope, and Love inspired me to fully embrace my true self and allowed me to open the door to all the blessings that came. That's what I want and wish for everyone who needs and wants their light to shine. And that's the Why of this book.

Unbeknownst to my parents, before I was five years old, I had faced repeated sexual abuse by members of our extended family. At barely seven, I inherited the responsibility of a parent, and bore the ridicule and bullying of being "abnormal," for by fifth grade I was already five feet eleven inches. Added to this, I came from a striving family with a lack mentality and one that faced disruptive medical conditions. Entrepreneurial and determined to break away from a disturbing past, everyone in our household had a role to play in securing the success of the family unit. Mine was to help take care of the needs of my immediate family.

Nothing about this seemed out of the ordinary in my household. This was our life. But my psyche understood its needs, and through flight, fight, faint, or fawn, it tried to survive. I did all of the above as a child to remain mentally healthy. My childhood psyche held on to so many things that didn't feel loving, rendering me with feelings of shame, fear, guilt, and very low self-esteem. Too young to fully understand what my mind couldn't explain, I took on self-protective behaviors and retreated into a shell that kept people at bay. This also kept my parents from understanding how vulnerable and distraught I truly was on the inside as a child.

It's only as an adult that I found the courage to crawl out of the self-imposed protective shell and the strength and freedom to call my childhood self into existence. Everything I am writing in this book as it relates to my childhood is a haze of recall because as a child I was so suppressed and compartmentalized, going through the motions of living, but on the inside, I was suffering to the point of numbness. Editing out experiences too scary to remember is a natural human instinct to self-protect and armor up to go into the world and continue.

From my emotionally challenged life, you might ask how I got to the point of understanding and forgiveness. I can only tell you what I believe were the ordered steps of my soul calling me home. At its core, whether I believed it or not, was love. In whatever form it took, I was cherished, and it was that kernel of hope that had me kicking and screaming to be heard despite my feelings of invisibility or the temptation to remain disassociated from my life.

My search for living with and giving unconditional love is the story I share with you in this book. It is my remembrance journey of returning to innocence and the pure loving essence of my soul. In recounting my life, I experienced significant pain and struggle, but I hope you will come to see I have no regrets. I have claimed and continue to claim my daily happiness and through Faith, Hope, Love, and hard work, I have landed in a place where my gifts have been set free.

Ultimately, my story is about love, about moving beyond the protective shell I created around pain, fear, and hopelessness to rediscover peace, love, joy, and indeed inner light. The question I kept asking myself when nothing I was doing helped me to feel good, was what is my purpose for being here? I would come to know life is teaching us all the time. My story is about finding and aligning with my purpose. It is a roadmap to the remembrance of me, and how I found my way through the pain, fear, and suffering to unconditional love as my state of being. Unconditional love eclipsed my pain and hurt and allowed me to put down the burden of shame, guilt, anger, and self-loathing. Loving myself connected me to grace, and compassion allowing my connection to the divine and to the ultimate freedom I sought. Self-love.

It turns out for me, the keys to unlocking my door to fulfillment were Faith, Hope, Love. Wrap your head around the esoteric concept that all things happen for a purpose; it doesn't matter that you don't like or understand what's happening, just know it's happening for a reason, conspiring to bring your spirit into full view. The spiritual threads of Faith, Hope, and Love are what connect us to the root of our pain as well as our joy. They help to uncover parts of ourselves that are buried, and they create space to see the beauty and goodness in all things. As Maslow so aptly stated, once our basic needs are met, the soul might seek to go on a journey of self-actualization

This book is for anyone who has felt or feels they cannot rise above their circumstances to a place of Glorious Arising and into full beingness. Let me define what I have come to understand after a ten-year journey into self about Faith, Hope, and Love; the triad keys that opened the doors to my fulfillment, self-harmony, universal truth, and clarity. These keys have propelled me along my journey to the remembrance of who I truly am and though they might resonate differently with you, their ultimate function will be the same—a discovery of self that will never leave you the same.

Faith is the illumination of our minds to a truth we did not see before.

Hope is an awakening of the heart that brings our feelings into our awareness.

Love is an action of connection. Love connects faith and hope, what you see and what you feel into an understanding of how you are connected or disconnected with all you want for yourself.

My journey is in the context of these three pillars and I will share with you later in the book, examples of how they showed up in my life. Let me start at the beginning of my story to share the life that inevitably led me to where I am now. Living in a place of Grace, and filled with Faith, Hope, Love, Joy, and indeed Peace. I can't wait for what is to come in the next chapters of my life.

Faith, Hope, and Love,
Kiana Webb

CHAPTER ONE
LOCKED

☥

I WAS BORN INTO a survivor's story. Geraldine Renee and Reginald Webb are my parents. My mom's maiden name is Brown, and she was raised by a single mother, Amelia Geraldine, (we call her Nana though she went by Jerry).

Nana had four children, two boys and two girls. My mom is the youngest of the four. When my mom was just weeks old my grandfather, Edgar Guy Brown, took her three siblings and moved to California, telling Nana he would come back and get her and the baby. That was the last time my mom would see him for over fourteen years, though she would meet him when she was three years old when the courts summoned him for child support delinquency. On his way to California, Granddaddy left his other daughter, Aunty Sandra with relatives in Nebraska and continued on to California with his sons. It was almost a year before Nana found out her older daughter was not with her husband. She immediately set out to get my Aunty Sandra. Nana divorced Granddaddy Brown when Mom was four and they moved to a basement apartment in the slums of Boston, and as my mother tells it, with rats and all. In 1960, Nana remarried Daddy Scott and moved back to Medford to a much nicer neighborhood, but Nana was always searching for a life of love and fulfillment by the world's standards.

Nana had no choice but to push back against her limitations. And Nana was incredible. Remember, this was in the '40s, '50s, and '60s when African Americans were not given positions of prestige. Yet, my Nana was able to work for companies such as Raytheon, where she could move up in the ranks and serve powerful people in the organization. Busy, Nana nonetheless raised her daughters to be independent and able to fend for themselves.

My mom took these lessons to heart. She was born in 1950 in Medford, Massachusetts as Geraldine Rene, but everyone called her Rene. Having a lot of responsibilities thrust upon her, even though she was the youngest, she was the most responsible by far. At an early age beginning around seven, my mom would take a train and a bus across multiple towns from downtown Boston into Medford though she was afraid of public transportation. Mom took life seriously and found a way to live with life's disappointments. At a young age, she found the church, found God, and dedicated her life to His work. No matter what she was doing, Mom never lost sight of her love of God; the foundation of her ability to navigate life's challenges.

Mom's life to say the least was challenging. She lived a latchkey life where she constantly fought with her older sister until her mother told her she was physically bigger and that was that. Abandoned by her father and her mother's divided loyalty to multiple marriages, Mom learned how to navigate the landscape of uncertainty. She learned how to self-protect from her mom's multiple husbands, one who was no less a pastor who spent Saturday nights in drinking revelry and went to church on Sundays to preach with conviction. Mom's instincts to assess people were honed to a tee. Her upbringing was helped along by the Boys and Girls Club which provided food, toys, and exposure she wouldn't have had in her community.

Mom was naturally bright and excelled in school. She was put on a college-bound track and attracted the attention of many schools, believing she could attend Harvard like two of her cousins did. With God's guidance, her internal fortitude, and her friends, Mom never went down the path that her circumstances may have dictated. She had goals and set her sights on achieving them, always driven to be her best self. Through it all, she somehow learned the value of honoring her space and making sure she was taken care of one way or the other. Shrewd as a snake, and seemingly gentle as a lamb, Mom had a wry sense of humor. She loved to dance, was fairly well-traveled, given the times, feisty, self-sufficient, indefatigable, not too trusting, prudent, and militant

Possibly hoping for a reconciliation, and because Granddaddy Brown had promised to help with her education at fifteen, Nana sent Mom to spend a summer with him. Granddaddy Brown had never changed and still loved his women. That summer he took Mom to Hawaii with him. A 'playa' with an amazing gift to weave and craft stories, though he was fun to be around, many would say he was a con man. When my mom was approached on the island by an older man who offered to take care of her, her father encouraged it. Disgusted, Mom knew, how to draw the line instinctively sensing that going with him would end in disaster, and soon returned to her mother in Boston before returning to California at sixteen in 1966. Her father had again promised to foot the bill for her college education.

Born in South Bend, Indiana in 1948 to a young mother, Reginald Webb was raised by his grandmother, Mama Annie and surrounded by her love from the time he was an infant. There was one interesting story about this. Mamma Matt, Mattie to her friends, my dad's Mom, became pregnant from Mama Annie's "friend" of the time. It could have been the reason she took him in as her own, but that's unverified. Dad's mother would later marry and have four other children, two boys and two girls, when Dad was still a toddler. Reginald always felt like an outsider to his immediate family, to the point of even being called a bastard, but because of his grandma, he always felt a sense of belonging.

Materially poor, dad was reserved, held everything close to his vest, and found it hard to share his feelings. Yet Momma Annie had instilled in him his own sense of greatness. A phenomenal orator, dad was brilliant and could influence relationships. He saw patterns, opportunities, and the big picture when others could not.

At ten years old, in what seemed a rite of passage for all the children, my dad was sent to the South for a year to help on the farm of family members still into raising crops. He'd entered a world of racial separation he'd not quite seen before and shared stories of having to walk a mile around the white school to get to the black school…because he could not take a shortcut through the white school. There were white water fountains and colored water fountains, yet he adapted but never lost his sense of purpose. On the farm, he was taught to produce from the land all that was necessary for the family. He picked cotton and suffered the indignities of racial segregation.

The next year, he and his grandmother moved to South Central Los Angeles where his father had already relocated. Moving to LA was not the wrong move but his father was so mean to both him and his grandma, Mama Annie moved them into one room in a boarding house where they had to share a bathroom with three other families. My father grew up poor but was never poor in spirit, and his outlook on life was always hopeful. He was taught to work hard, solve problems, and to find a way out of no way. Like mom, he never had a relationship with his father not even as he grew older. But he was not one to look back on shortcomings or misfortunes. Through strong and deep values inculcated by his grandmother, he like mom forged ahead steering clear of the stereotype of single-parent households. Through his belief in himself and determination, dad would chart the life he lived. And he succeeded.

When dad was eighteen, he met mom who was sixteen. Unbeknownst to her, they had been set up on a blind date by my father's cousin. Mom had believed she was meeting the cousin, but the cousin, it seemed, felt my mom was a perfect fit for my dad. When dad met mom, she had already been on her own and fully aware that if she would make it in this life, she could only depend on herself. However, firm as she was in her decision to make it on her own, he was a breath of fresh air.

To shore up his direction, after graduating high school, dad joined the U.S. Coast Guard and upon honorable discharge began his work in earnest of making communities better. Dad had been working for the poverty program, always giving back because it was the life he knew, and that could have sat well with my God-loving mother. But he also had an entrepreneurial mindset and was constantly trying to figure out how to help others come along as he was being built up.

Something about dad kepy mom's interest. Maybe it was the dimple puckering her cheeks, or the fact that she is beautiful, but if you asked him he would say it was her thick thighs. My father, too, was quite the catch, handsome and ambitious. Mom would wait for him. They might have sensed in each other an indomitable force and a few years after he was discharged from the Coast Guard they married. My parents married when she was twenty-one and he was twenty-three. Dad began working with the Greater LA Community Action Agency, but when my older brother was about to be born in 1974, he decided a job that was going to allow him to take care of his family was needed, and in 1973, applied for the McDonald's Management Training Program. Our family moved to Oak Brook, Illinois as a part of his training program when I was one year old.

During his training, the first store he managed was a McDonald's restaurant in California, and he loved California. His rise in McDonald's was meteoric. At the time he joined them, there weren't a lot of Black executives and very few throughout the '70s and '80s had ascended the ranks my father had. With his natural gift of bringing people together and of seeing beyond what was being said, to what was being thought, dad had great leadership qualities. He could paint a vision for others of how to create a life they could see for themselves. The way he spoke and still speaks about things has always been captivating for the people he worked with. The people under his charge felt empowered to share what they most wanted for their lives and together, as a cohesive team they created magic.

Dad rose in rank and as a McDonald's executive he was gone a lot. Traveling all over the country he'd only come home on Fridays and leave again Sunday night or Monday morning. Seeing my dad on Fridays when he would walk through the door was such a gift because I loved him so much. I still do. When my dad came home it was like sunshine came back into the house. I would run to him and wrap my arms around his legs as he tried to maneuver me through the house. And the thing is, I was young, but I was tall and not very lightweight. Being young, I was acting my age, but I was also probably hurting him when I would stand on his feet, and he would take a few steps forward. Then he would bend down, hug me, and say, "Okay, Kiana, let me say hello to your mom."

The most memorable moments of my childhood and my favorite were when I would lie on the sofa with my dad. I would put my head on his chest, and he would just hold me as we watched TV. We could be there for hours, and it didn't matter what we were watching because I wasn't watching anything but basking in every loving moment of just being held. I didn't realize at the time how much I needed his reassurance. Being held "just because" is probably one of my favorite things in the whole world, even today.

Several years later, in 1985, he became the owner of two McDonald's restaurants in Pomona, California. It was also the year Kyle, my younger brother, was born. A few months before his birth, dad decided to leave his corporate job as a VP of McDonald's and the regional Officer in Southern California which included Hawaii, and become a full-time franchisee. Dad had experienced and witnessed many injustices and wanted to create real change for his family and for others working in the corporate world who were not fully allowed to show their best. He felt becoming a franchisee gave him the ability to pass his wealth on to his kids. Unlike a job, he would be able to pass on ownership, which meant something very different in terms of legacy, making an impact, and breaking down barriers.

So, when my dad left corporate life where he worked eighty-hour weeks and came home full-time, I thought it was going to be great. What I didn't get was how he'd disrupt every routine and every system my mom had in place for the past seven years. It was interesting to watch my parents navigate who was responsible for what, now my dad was home. Our household was strictly patriarchal so when dad was home, my very independent mom acquiesced to his control, as did we, kids.

Our life of comfort also changed. We went from walking into large hotel suites, sometimes two stories with a conference table, a grand piano, a kitchen, and multiple bedrooms to staying at Holiday Inn, barely able to afford to go on vacations. It was such a big shift going from never having my parents worry about food to my mom sometimes staring into almost bare cupboards, trying to figure out how to make a meal out of whatever was there. I remember watching my mom crying, sometimes in fear or maybe frustration, trying to figure out how we were going to continue to afford the life we had been used to. My mom would pray a lot with her Bible always open on her lap as they navigated their life as parents, as individuals, as business partners, and as husband and wife. But he had a plan.

The moment he began expanding his McDonald's restaurants I found us moving back into our historical patterns. The only difference was Mom stopped her bookkeeping company and became the accountant and administrator responsible for all the back-office services for our restaurants. We became a family where everyone was involved, and we all worked in our business.

Having earned her accounting degree from Cal State, LA, Mom had been running her own company, Prosperous Horizons, working from home. She did the books for many businesses, and before that worked for the Gas Company as an accountant. So, in 1985, when we became McDonald's franchise owners my life again significantly shifted; even though he came home every day my dad was again gone all the time. Alongside each other, through sheer ambition, grit, and hard work they built a life that afforded their family a solid upper-middle-class upbringing and in time made the business a true family affair.

With guidance from dad and the help of family, the company grew into seventeen franchises across two counties, from Baldwin Park to Colton including in the cities of Claremont, La Puente, Montclair, Ontario, and San Bernardino, Pomona, West Covina, and later expanding into other holdings. On the move, daddy earned his pilot's license which gave him a sense of accomplishment and freedom. He sat on many boards in the process, creating a life for his children far from the one he knew in his childhood. This, to him, was his love in action.

Growing up as a Webb has always been special. People have told me this my entire life. "You are very privileged being a Webb," they'd say. And I would think, well, that's all I know, so I don't know what it means to be privileged. What I do know is, that we Webbs worked hard. Every weekend, my dad would have us working in the yard and as we got older, we would go to work at McDonald's. We hired someone to live with us Monday through Friday to help my mom with stuff that needed to be done as all the responsibility of the children fell to her. On Saturdays, the helper would go home to her family and my mom would do her work the best she could from home.

Mom's first symptoms of MS happened when she was in her late teens or early twenties but were so minor, they were not diagnosed. After a few doctors' visits and no diagnosis, it wasn't until 1982 that she was officially diagnosed with MS. With much prayer and patience, her symptoms abated, and she rebounded. Elated, they decided to have another child. Mom gave birth to my brother, Kyle, in 1985. Shortly after they came home from the hospital, she had a massive flare-up and was in a lot of pain, becoming bedridden for a while. It was the beginning of the end of my life as I had known it.

When my younger brother was born, I was seven and a half years old. And I claim that half a year because it makes a difference for me. It was then that I emotionally, if not intellectually began to understand life for me would be dedicated to my family. By seven and a half, I had assumed the caregiver's role for my younger brother because it was how I could help my ailing mom. No one had asked me to do anything, but my sensing was, I could help.

One of my earliest memories of Mom in pain happened when I was five and a half. It was a hot, sticky day, and we'd spent the afternoon at my grandma's house. I was sitting in the back seat of our rust-colored Volvo and dad had just pulled into the driveway of our home. I'd been excited to get out of the sweaty car because my legs were sticking to the dark upholstery of the backseat. Suddenly, my mom started shaking and moaning in the passenger seat. My concern for my comfort was gone and I shouted, "Mom! Mom! Are you okay?"

I was terrified hearing my mom in so much pain. Not knowing what to do, I froze. I was so scared of losing my mom. Dad began calling her name, repeatedly. I watched helplessly as she contorted in on herself, her arms and hands shaking and drawing in. Her moaning and groaning scared me more than anything I had ever heard before. I didn't know what to do, but I wanted it to stop. And it didn't stop; it just kept going and going. I had to get out of there. I unbuckled my seatbelt, opened the car door, and ran. I could faintly hear mom saying to dad, "Go help Kiana, it's gonna be okay. Just go help Kiana," as I ran away from my mom's hurting. I ran from my helplessness. When I finally realized where I was, I was standing in the middle of the street with my hands over my ears and tears rolling down my face. Looking back at my car, my house, and my family, I saw my dad racing toward me with a terrified look on his face.

"Kiana! Don't move," he swooped me up and held me tight to his chest as we ran back toward the car. Without letting me go, he opened the front passenger door, crouched down, and wrapped his free arm around mom's shaking body. For what felt like hours but was probably only five minutes, my dad held us both as best as he could. I felt his helplessness. His fear. His sorrow. When the seizure finally ended, weak and visibly shaken, we helped my exhausted mom into the house and into bed. As my dad softly closed the door to their room, he turned to me and said what would come to define the next thirty years of my life.

"Kiana," he said. "We just need to help Mommy. I know it's going to be hard, but we just need to help her. It's gonna be okay."

My dad was visibly upset and all I could think of was wanting to be able to fix it, to help my parents in any way I could. With a feeling of helplessness, we left the room.

My parents had a large master bedroom. I vividly remember the room. As you walked in, their bed was to the right, and next to it was a dresser. To the left and up a few stairs were his and hers bathrooms, separate closets with a shower that connected them. To the right of the room was a sitting area with a bay window and two blue recliners. I remember sitting in one of those chairs holding my brother for hours. I could feel such beautiful loving energy coming from him into me, but by this time I had lost my sense of love. I had lost my center. I couldn't tell you then why that was, but I can now. Little did I know then I was holding a light bearer in my arms.

Once my mom gained trust I was going to be okay taking care of my brother, she allowed me to take him for walks around the upstairs area. Eventually, I could go downstairs with him, and I'd just hold on to this light being, this beautiful expression of innocence, of purity, of just absolute unconditional love and trust. I would sit with him for hours and hours absorbing his pure energy. My little brother was so cute and for the rest of my childhood, until I left for college, he became a light that helped me navigate some of the dark challenges of my life.

Because I was responsible and could take care of things, or maybe because I was the only girl, my parents asked a lot of me. I began to give my all to my family and I learned to shelve my needs and hide from my pain. Relieved there was something I could do to help mom, I settled into my new role as my brother's caregiver and my family's supporter. That day a new Kiana was born. The adult Kiana who took care of everyone, the Kiana child who was repeatedly being abused, and the sad and lonely Kiana no one knew.

When mom had difficulty getting out of bed during her flares, dad pushed her to overcome. Mom would have good months and bad months. When she was doing well I helped as much as possible so she didn't overdo it and cause her disease to flare. When she was in a flare, I would try to do everything so she could rest.

I'll never forget one time soon after my brother was born; Mom was having such a hard time and probably feeling guilty she couldn't take care of my brother the way she wanted, and my dad said to me, "Your mom is hurting. Don't bother her." I was doing all I could to help, and I interpreted his comment as don't be a bother to your mother, so I rarely asked questions. That prodded my limiting beliefs. The last thing I wanted to be was a bother. I stopped asking for help even when she was doing well. Even then I knew I could never share the secret of my ongoing abuse and I became the child who would just figure it out. I figured out how to change diapers. I figured out how to clean up after my family and I helped my brother as much as I could since I still had to go to school. And I endured adult things I should not have.

By this time, my mom had fully acquiesced to my father's patriarchal style and her job was to keep us in line when he was home. My dad is a very picky eater, and he loves food, but if it isn't prepared to his liking, well he just won't touch it. My mom taught me how to cook the basics for our family and especially how to cook for him. After a while, I could cook full meals. So, I learned how to cater to needs: his needs, her needs, the needs of my brothers, and anyone else who needed my help.

While dad enjoyed the accolades of a successful titan, it was with mom's help, who leaned on me heavily, who made sure everything worked behind the scenes. As a powerful and super independent person, though she soldiered on because that's what dad expected, MS had robbed her of so much. Trying to rise above her illness prevented her from going down the rabbit hole of self-pity and made her take charge of her disease in ways she might not have. I never knew when my mom slipped from being the strong, determined woman she'd always been to conforming to the patriarchal household my father had established and great-grandmother Momma Annie demanded.

CHAPTER TWO
MY STORY

☥

IF YOU CAN HAVE a debilitating but good life at the same time, that's what I've had. Suppressed, I don't have many memories before I was five years old. To me, that's strange because I remember tangible things like my parents' playing cards and dominoes and sharing a grand time with our extended family, eating, and having fun. I also remember what our kitchen looked like in Oakbrook, Illinois, with its dark brown cabinets and the shaggy green carpet of the attached living room. I also remember my older cousin, Kira, who I followed everywhere, and most of the people in my life, but beyond that, emotionally, nothing. I don't remember if I was happy or sad back then, but I'd bet the latter. Intellectually, I have always known I was loved but despite that, for as far back as I can remember, I was always a sad and lonely child. As an adult, I had a recall which could have been the root of my blocking memory. I have no actual knowledge if this is true or not, but I remember when I first psychologically fainted. I was in meditation when a vision came to me. My family was at the Dodger Stadium, which happens to be my mom's favorite way of celebrating her birthday. Both my parents and my older brother Karim were there. My dad was sitting to the right of me three rows down facing the field. Karim was sitting two rows down and slightly to the right of me, and Mom was one row ahead of me to the right, but not as far over as my dad, maybe about five or six seats in. I was sitting in the aisle staring at the back of their heads and Mom's side profile. A fog obscured anything beyond the seating a few rows past my dad. My mom appeared to be doing a full summersault in her chair and just kept spinning and spinning. I couldn't understand what Mom was doing and just stared at her. Finally, my brother said, "Kiana, go help mom!"

I was thinking all the time why didn't he do it as he was closer to her? As I went to touch her, suddenly I was transported to my grandma's bedroom. On the bed under the covers was this movement and somehow, I felt compelled to help. I go toward the bed and grab the cover. The people turned over and I was staring at my father's mother Mamma Matt, and a young girl who was about three or four years old with my mother's face. And when I really looked at her, I realized it was me. "That's me," I said, and the moment I acknowledged it this rush of energy left my body and it felt so good, I immediately woke up fully feeling an opening to freedom within and joy. It brought back a memory of Momma Annie shouting at Momma Matt asking her what she was doing to me. From then on, I was never allowed to be alone with Momma Matt. I told my cousin Kira, and she did not seem surprised, and we cried together about it. After the vision, I stopped disassociating. I knew I needed healing. As I would later find out; in my direct line both rape and molestation were a part of our history.

I was born in January 1978. By the age of two, my pediatrician said I would be over six feet and indeed I have been six feet two inches since eighth grade. I am the middle child and the only girl of my parents' three children. I am not true to the Middle Child Syndrome, in fact, maybe just the opposite. I was never overly rebellious or competitive. For most of my life, except for a stint in Chicago, I have lived on the East LA county border before it reaches San Bernardino County. Our life mimicked the words Martin Luther King espoused, "I have a dream that my four little children will one day live in a nation where they will not be judged by the color of their skin, but by the content of their character."

My community in Rowland Heights was just the kind of neighborhood he talked about. It wasn't just a community of white families and Black families; the whole world was represented there. An upper-middle-class neighborhood, it was a true multicultural enclave. My next-door neighbors from the west to the east were what we called the shades because I lived on a street where my neighbors to the right were Chinese, to the left Latinx, across the street Caucasians replete with red hair and blue eyes, and next to them, a lesbian Asian couple. We were the African Americans on our street, but there were other African American families in the neighborhood. Our neighbor to the east had three daughters. The youngest, Melissa, and I used to play together quite often until we got a little older. Around the corner were the Blanco's. Their daughter Nicole was one of my best friends growing up and she had a brother Richie. Across the street were the Rankins, who had two boys and a girl. The entire family had the brightest auburn-colored hair and blue eyes. We would all play together, and it never dawned on me it wasn't normal because that was just our life.

As a community we would come together and have block parties where we closed the street to the chagrin of the police officer who would come and be mad saying, we couldn't do it, *wink, wink*, because we didn't have a permit. The incredible thing is, the wonderful Asian ladies who everyone knew were gay, were treated no differently from anyone else in the neighborhood. And though they were quiet and didn't engage much, they always participated in our community gatherings. It was a neighborhood where everyone looked out for each other. When the lights dimmed at night, neighbors would send us home saying, "Hey, be careful." Even as the neighborhood grew, our little world remained a safe haven.

As a family, we looked forward to visiting our relatives in LA, where, lest we forget, Karim and I would get a good dose of Black culture from our African American, cousins, aunts, grandmother, and great-grandmother. It was a spirited and a great time. My parents would effortlessly ease right back into the culture in which they grew up. Playing cards, Bid Wiz, was a favorite, but Spades was not their thing. Then they would be "throwing down the bones" playing dominoes as they say in Black vernacular. That meant talking a lot of "hot mess" and reminiscing as extended family and friends dropped by my grandmother's house to greet us. There'd be loud music playing, and amazing soul food being cooked, with, of course, mac and cheese, greens, southern fried chicken, and oxtail. My great-grandmother, Momma Annie, would sometimes cook chitlins, which for me were quite disgusting. Added to the mix were candied yams, sweet potato pies, and a whole lot of other desserts.

I loved watching my great-grandmother cook because she always did it with love. She loved feeding our family and we loved being together, surrounded by all that Black love. But when I went home, I was surrounded by universal love, so, I've always had the perspective of cultural fluency no matter where I've gone or what situation I find myself in. Living in Rowland Heights helped shape my perspective that all people had the same human experiences and needs. It didn't matter what language we spoke at home or what our cultural differences were, we all wanted the same thing: love, contentment, prosperity, and the ability to stay safe in our environment. Having a multicultural perspective was helpful to me as I navigated the business world I inhabited.

Growing up, I only felt comfortable being alone. Before I became invisible, I thought nothing of it, but as I grew up, I could no longer intellectually ignore reality, even though emotionally I had donned my invisible cloak. I would always be surprised when I walked into a room and said something that stopped all conversations. How could that be when I was invisible?

Because I adored my dad, I wanted very much to please him, so I'd do anything he asked. My dad adored me too and this might have caused my mother some angst which in turn plucked my guilt when my great-grandmother used to say, "Oh here comes Kiana. She's Reggie's heart." For me it was great to hear because I knew it and because I felt it. I felt how much my dad loved me in more ways than he could ever show. When I was in high school and college we'd go on father-daughter "dates" where he would take me to eat, we would talk about life, and I would learn from him how he thought and analyzed information. Dad would pick me up in his plane and fly me to lunch in a nearby city and then bring me back. This was especially true when I was at college in San Francisco. There were times when I doubted my mom loved me, and understandably with all she had to deal with, there was an emotional distance from us kids.

Mom really wanted to be my dad's heart at a time when I didn't know he could reciprocate in the way he would have liked and she needed. He was working eighty-hour weeks and leaving corporate McDonald's increased his responsibilities as an owner franchisee. I think it was easy for him to shower me with love because I was emotionally detached from outcomes and could go the distance which he termed "additive." These were qualities he valued in me and saw in himself. Whether he really saw me for who I was emotionally or saw me based on my potential as he challenged me with tasks he knew I could do, I don't know. What I do know is, that it's both Daddy's and Momma Annie's love that saved me when I faced my darkest moments. Of the three of us kids, by far I got most of the encouraging love my father had to give. Possibly unaware to him, it only came out when one was obedient or additive, which I was. My brother Karim would tell a far different story as obedience was not in his nature.

A Love Like No Other

My Great-grandma, Momma Annie, was born and raised in Mississippi in the early 1900s to parents who were sharecroppers. Striving was her life. Full of her convictions, she'd forged ahead in her life, doing what she thought needed to be done, most often with good results which probably reinforced her belief in self. Despite opposition she single-handedly pulled her family out of poverty, moving them across the country to a place that offered the best opportunity to prosper. As a young woman, she quickly realized her family would go nowhere if they stayed in Mississippi. Firm in her belief, she convinced most of her twelve younger siblings to move with her during what is now called the Great Migration. They originally ended up in Indiana but soon realized other places would offer better opportunities. Momma Annie packed up her family once again and moved to LA, where she steadily built community and relationships within her immediate and extended family, church, and neighborhood. My father adored and admired his grandmother and was determined to make her proud. Mamma Annie's, quite the matriarch, control over dad was significant. Dad, she knew, could carry the family torch further down the road and she saw him as the way out of poverty for her family lineage. Momma Annie would control any and everything that stood in her grandson's way, including my mom whom she had groomed to be the partner he needed.

I remember sitting on the counter in her kitchen with its old *Leave It to Beaver* stove and flowered wallpaper, swinging my legs and knocking my heels against the lower cupboards. Flour would be swirling in the air as her strong, gnarled hands expertly kneaded dough about to become our dessert. I would help Momma Annie snap green peas banging my feet against the counter.

"Stop that racket!" She'd bark at me as she focused on placing the dough in the oiled bowl for its first rise. I only got fresh pies at Momma Annie's house, and I was excited to eat them. The dress she wore that day looked the opposite of how she seemed to me. It was a soft pink with muted flowers. It had short sleeves and hung down well past her knees. Under the skirt, her slip was peeking out on one side and was snagged on her thick stockings. But what I saw was a solid mountain of a woman who knew who she was and what she wanted, despite her soft dress. She believed beyond doubt, everything would be all right. Yes indeed, my great-grandmother was a force to be reckoned with. She was tough as nails but also loved grandly. With faith, strength, grit, and tenacity she conquered her dreams for her family and passed those qualities of determination on to my father, on to my mother, and on to their great-grandchildren.

Momma Annie's directness and stubbornness could, and often did, offend people but she didn't care to mind anyone else's business but her own. Unlike me, she always said what she felt, but like me, she didn't always have to be talking. When she did, she didn't mince words, and most of the time, the truth she spoke could be construed as mean. "Honey, you are dumb if you think that boy you're dating is going to take you anywhere in life. He is only going to drag you down." One of the amazing things to me about Momma Annie was her sense of security and superior self-esteem.

Like her grandson, Momma Annie was a community builder and was devoted to my dad, to me, to Jesus, to her family, and her community. From Momma Annie, I learned the strength of conviction. The one thing I *didn't* learn from Momma Annie was how to speak up when I was in pain or when I wanted to be heard. She passed away when I was twenty-two years old and I miss her to this day. Momma Annie believed in me. She loved me, protected me, and accepted me as I was, with all my flaws and gifts. She saw them and called them out, but never condemned me for my shortcomings and always praised me for my gifts.

By the time I was in sixth grade, at five feet eleven inches, I was the tallest person in the school, and that included the principal who was a gangly man. My physicality, of course, led to many incidents. I can't tell you how many comments I endured like, "You're just too tall for a girl, " or "How is the weather up there?" With feet too big and legs too long for girl shoes and clothing, I remember how hard my mom tried to make me feel "normal," but it wasn't enough for the lost little girl going through the motions of being an adult, doing adult things and carrying adult secrets while still just a little girl. The funny thing about all this is, because I'm a fixer, I could have easily made friends; I just didn't want to. I didn't want being me: the way I spoke, the vocabulary I used, my height, or my general disposition, to be topics of conversation.

For whatever reason, I was who I was, and I couldn't change it. I didn't necessarily love it at the time, but neither did I have a desire to fit in. This further drove me into isolation. My mom used to say, "Man, I wish Kiana had friends," or "Kiana don't you want to go and play with the neighbors or play with someone."

No, I didn't. I couldn't have cared less about being part of the crowd and I certainly wasn't feeling encouraged to try. This meant I spent a lot of time with myself, and I loved it! It wasn't that I had much time on my hands with all my responsibilities, but when I did, I rather loved spending it in my room reading. I had a real passion for books, and my books became my good and dependable friends. In second through third grade Judy Blume's, and the other books I loved plumbed my imagination while letting me explore people's lives and worlds on their black and white pages. Romance novels, which I later graduated to, offered the kind of passionate love I never saw at home. But what seemed like love in my cocoon were walls of protection.

I suppose growing up as the only girl with two boys might have led to a sense of loneliness, but my loneliness was far from gender issues—I felt wounded. How did I find my joy in my dark hole? In how I interacted within my world. I'd find myself doing a lot for other people, and because I was a fixer, there were a lot of people and things in need of fixing. When I didn't want to, and didn't have the capacity to say no, I would detach myself from everything. Even on the playground, I had no problem being by myself. Sitting against the school building I would watch everyone playing, with zero regrets. I might have numbed out to external influences, but I did have one friend who I really liked, Esther. She was just so great. She was Chinese and she had this amazing dimple on the side of her mouth. I liked her dimple because my mom has one, but Esther's was deep, and it was something that once again reminded me people are the same no matter their culture. We were remarkably similar, and our friendship was quiet. We used to talk about her dimple a lot and we bonded over *Hello Kitty. I* didn't feel overwhelmed playing with Esther, she belonged in my tribe for whatever reason.

Esther and I did a lot on the monkey and parallel bars at school. I remember being able to do flips and tricks, mastering the bars with ease. At one point when I'd agreed to engage, there was such fearlessness about me when I was playing, I wished I could have bottled it up instead of hunching over to diminish my height. Because of my size and abilities as a natural athlete, everybody in PE class wanted me on their team; depending on the sport. No one wanted me if the game was soft or dainty, but if rough and tumble like basketball, baseball, kickball, or flag football, I was one of the first to be picked.

It was in elementary school too that I came face-to-face with racial hatred. In the fifth grade, I had a teacher who just didn't like me. I couldn't fathom what I had done to earn her vitriol, so I sucked it up and shrunk back into myself. Toward the end of the fifth grade, I was really struggling in school. No matter what I did I couldn't get good grades. I felt very alienated and angry, and my self-esteem slipped further. I'd gotten good grades when my teachers were great, but I didn't fare well under this teacher's outward hatred of me. One day she finally said something that made me snap. I don't remember exactly what was said but I was upset. When I got home, I told my parents just how awfully this teacher had been treating me. Because of my response to her, I'd been sent to the principal, and they were going to suspend me and send me home. A part of me was elated to see my fighting spirit emerge, reminding me I was alive and breathing but there was a much greater part of me that was afraid, and I didn't want to disappoint my parents. Still, my outburst showed I was not just coasting through life emotionless. When the principal called my mom, she hightailed it down to the school. During the meeting, the teacher began telling her all the stuff about me that was wrong. It was a private school, so they didn't have to follow the Department of Education process. Mid-conversation, my mom excused me from the meeting. Outside, I could see her fuming. She looked at the principal and asked how could the school allow a teacher to talk so derogatorily about a student. That was my last year there.

I'd spent my entire year in fifth grade under the auspices of hate and as I said, it further eroded my self-esteem. Since I couldn't explain or understand why I was being mistreated it was yet another reason to turn inward. I was trying to explain to my parents the teacher was just plain racist, but because of the times, clearly not the 40s, 50s, or 60s, there was a disconnect with what I was sharing. I didn't want to be a bother anymore, and yes, in the 80s overt racism was alive and well. My mother, however, seemed to harbor the idea my rebelling was a sign of life. I remember in high school when it was senior ditch day I was not feeling well so I left school to go home. I had called my mom who thought I was going home because I was ditching. So proud, she called all her family and said, "Guess what, Kiana is ditching!" She was sorely disappointed when she found out the reason I'd ditched school was because I was sick!

The fifth grade proved to be quite the year that pummeled and sealed my protective container. The final straw happened because my mom decided to change her hair stylist for a brief period. Since my hair was an asset, thick and long, and differentiated me as a girl I went with her to the hair salon. I truly had lovely hair and with it coiffed no one could dare mistake me for anything but a girl, despite my height. To my horror, the beautician I was assigned left the curl product on my hair too long and fried it. Over the next few days, my beautiful hair turned grey and began to fall out. I looked terrible and had to cut my hair. So here I am, about 5'10, maybe 5'11, in the fifth grade with my hair cut into a really, really short natural. This is back in the '80s when short naturals on females were not in vogue. During my "bald" period everywhere I went, it didn't matter whether I was wearing earrings or a dress, I was always mistaken for a boy. It was beyond annoying. It didn't help either that no one in the area carried shoes or clothes for tall, young girls, or tall women for that matter. So, I was forced to wear men's shoes and men's pants most of the time. If I wanted a feminine look, I'd shop the petite section in a women's clothing store. I'd try on long, floor-length skirts which would be knee length on me. My mom did her best to help me feel pretty and feminine and she was supportive and sensitive to my plight. Mom would spend a hundred and fifty to two hundred dollars on shoes for me from a shoe store called Ruston's, which was the only shoe store that sold shoes for women with larger-sized feet. But they were adult shoes. They weren't designed for young girls. And so, you know, I was always in the contradictory position of being a young child in an adult body looking and behaving older than I was.

When I would go out with my mom, people would always say, "Oh, my gosh, your son is so handsome," or "Your son is so beautiful." One particular time, mom had asked me to go shopping with her I was wearing an outfit I got from the well-known petite clothing store where I shopped; it was quite girlie, and I loved it so much. It was purple, the shirt sweater had a light pink trim on the collar, sleeves, and on the waist area. The skirt, just above my knees, had a light pink trim and I felt all fluffy and friendly. I remember how proudly I put in matching pink ceramic animal earrings. Checking myself out in the mirror I thought I looked so cute. I was accompanying mom to buy a gift for someone's wedding or anniversary. We went into a store that does engraving and my mom handed the woman the gift.

"Your son is so handsome," says the woman.

"That's my daughter," my mom said.

"No, your son," the woman insisted.

"No. That's my daughter," mom says.

"OK," the woman nodded but for the third time said, "But your son is very good-looking."

Since there was no one else but mom and me, I couldn't understand her insistence. It was as if she could not comprehend that someone so tall could be a woman! Believe it or not, it still happens to me. Years later I was at the airport getting ready to go on a family vacation I walked into the bathroom and this woman started screaming at me.

"You're not supposed to be in here!" she leveled accusatory eyes.

I looked at her and said, "Yes, I am. You know I'm a woman, and I know because I have given birth to three children, two of them vaginally."

It's these types of comments I get to this day, because of my height. People still automatically assume I am a man, or I am an anomaly because of social conditioning. Can you imagine at twelve how I felt? I had internalized this; I was masculine; I wasn't attractive; I wasn't looked at as a love interest option for the kids who were my age. Things like those just made me keep to myself and I didn't allow people who I didn't trust or feel safe with around me, and so I continued to expand my boundary of protection.

Honestly, I had a lot of anger and resentment toward my mother. My thoughts were, had she not been sick I would not have been saddled with the life I had, and had she been able to stand up to my dad, my brother wouldn't have faced some of the hardships he did. For most of my growing-up years, it was far better to hide in my cocoon than to deal with the traumas of everyday living, and that's exactly what I did. From there, I worked hard to become who my family needed me to be. I doubled down on my detachment, and though I had my parents' love, I was still dealing with a lot of unspoken hurt. It didn't help. With all the internal turmoil I had to deal with, the external ones like having to wear boys' pants and men's shoes because of my height, the uncertainty of not knowing who I was took its toll emotionally.

From outsiders looking in, I should have been happy and joyous because I had a lot. My family could have been considered privileged with financial security and enviable opportunities. What they didn't see was the internal turmoil of dysfunction. Some might have coveted my height and the curvaceous figure I worked really hard to hide. Many people have often said I am pretty, regardless of whether they'd mistaken me as male or female. So why didn't I believe all this and why wasn't I happy or joyous? Societal "norm" meaning average, said I was too tall and therefore not attractive. And because my family was well-off, I had nothing to complain about.

It was my mother who made me play basketball in fifth grade and I played on three teams. I was actually good at it and excelled. But if you want to know the truth, I never really loved basketball as a sport but I learned some valuable lessons. The first time she took me to play basketball I was playing for a team on NJB (National Junior Basketball) league local to where I was in Diamond Bar. I was not enthused. I was good enough to coach for three years and one of my teams went from worst to best, which gave me an insight into who I truly was. As a team player, I leaned into my ability to help people win and move past their limitations. I learned if I was going to be successful while I was still uncertain, it would come in the form of a team effort.

Still, the thing I came to love about going to basketball practice was not the game but the community: my teammates, their families, and my coach. I really loved my coach, and I enjoyed playing and winning. But winning and playing were not about the sport but always about the people I could support. As many times as I've tried to explain this to others, they just couldn't get it, especially those who were sports fanatics listening to such a declaration from someone who lives in a cocoon!

I knew for sure when I got out of high school, I was college-bound. I was recruited to play on an AAU travel team. I was never playing for me but for others. While I was good, I never felt the need to play to my highest ability on the travel team because I didn't like my teammates, nor did I like my travel coach. Like in elementary school, it wasn't about camaraderie, but about what advantage I could provide for them as the tallest girl on the team as opposed to what we could create together. This should have been a clue that although I stayed in my cocoon my soul yearned for meaningful connections. And while I didn't believe I would have been able to articulate it that way then, I knew I was always holding myself back from my pure brilliance. For me, it's always about achieving with people who I care about.

Looking back, all of the things I do now and did then, from leading teams to supporting family, to helping anyone in need, really came from a place of connection. Creating a community, supporting a family, or creating a unit where everyone in their unique way contributed to their successes and outcomes beyond expectations, were my sweet spots. My hidden superpowers were setting and reaching goals as a team, and that's what I enjoyed. That's when I was useful; that's when I knew I could shine.

I remember when I would run down the basketball court in high school and my point guard, Kelly Chavez, would do a no look behind the neck pass and I would catch the ball and do this layup that had people amazed. It was like Showtime at the AMAT gym on my high school campus, and it was fun. I just really wanted to help my team win and to have everyone look good. I would feel like, "Oh, that was amazing." And that's really the essence of who I am, maximizing my team's effort. It was probably because that's who I've always been with my own family who worked hard together to accomplish a goal which was our communal success. Playing basketball with a team that didn't gel dampened my desire to shine.

I learned mostly to be average. It matched my invisibility. My passion was not around education and learning, and I would always get frustrated. The other me really wanted to be on the honor roll or have higher than a 3.3 GPA. My mother's badgering of making me repeatedly do my homework until it was perfect was to get me to be a star student and it took a toll on me. My teachers finally told her she was a part of my problem when I began withdrawing, and I was even sent to a psychologist. I was able to maintain my 3.3 GPA, but I wasn't a star student. I had no desire to stand out and simply wanted to fade away. I did learn one thing from this period of my life; I could do anything I put my mind to, and I wouldn't do anything I didn't want to.

I also learned a valuable lesson in high school, from my basketball coach, who was also the vice principal and who, although I didn't know it then, placed another rung on my ladder to claiming my joy. It was in my freshman year. My religion teacher, a nun, told me I was going to hell because I refused to convert to Catholicism. In so doing, she plucked at my need to be who I wanted to be, so I pushed back. This earned me a trip to the vice principal's office, who as I said was my basketball coach. A big advocate for me and my family, she gave me some sound advice I still think about to this day. She said, "Kiana, there are people who are so stuck in their beliefs. You'll never be able to change their minds. It's not your job to change their mind, but make sure what they say doesn't change yours. So, when you walk through this life, or into their class, specifically into her class, know what you need and don't make your principal's needs more important than your success. Don't get expelled because this teacher doesn't believe you are going to heaven, because that's something between you and God and that's it. Period."

That was very profound for me. It was telling me I didn't have to care about what others thought of me but what I thought of myself. It was overwhelming to think I was more than enough. You know, it's something I still reflect on to this day, and it's not just about, between me and God, it's between me and everything that stood in the way of my true self. Still, I was devoted to my family and especially to Kyle who truly felt like the light of my life.

Being on the varsity team, my last class of the day was PE. At 2:40 p.m. my coach would allow me to leave early to pick up my Kyle from school. I'd grab my gym bag, thank my coach, and sprint to my car. I'd think nothing of it as I cruised down the freeway to Kyle's school some twenty miles away to be there promptly as his school let out. I would then return to school, Kyle in tow, to attend my basketball practice before we headed home together. I was seventeen years old, but I'd been driving since I was twelve. I was always focused on being on time for everyone. I didn't have time to think about me, my pain, or my life in general.

Everyone has their way of dealing with their reality and mine was to disassociate. I didn't allow myself to feel, just to do. My spirit must have known its sacrifice by emotionally disassociating because I could easily put everyone's needs before my own, including shouldering my mother's displeasure and being her sounding board when my dad disappointed her. My life until my awakening was dedicated to my family.

That's why it hurts so much. With my brother's declaration, the chilly February day that had started like any other but by day's end had changed my life forever.

CHAPTER THREE
GROWING PAINS

MY LIFE HAD MOMENTS of genuine joy. I had a really good childhood and a really good life but there was a lot of pain in it that forced me to suppress my emotions. The net result left me with a lot of self-doubt, a lack of self-worth, low self-esteem, and a disconnection from my soul. Now spiritually aware I know what I experienced was colored by the lens through which I viewed my life. It was not that I didn't have love surrounding me, and it's not that I didn't know I was loved I just didn't feel it. I couldn't feel what love beyond obligations was meant to feel like. In my interpretation, love was only experienced when I did something for someone. In my child's mind, my role of giving and serving my family brought rewards and the feeling of being loved which I needed. These rewards and feelings were clearly enjoyable, but I rarely felt safe within myself. Love and safety were the highest on my list and many of those moments in my childhood came from time spent with my dad.

McDonald's represented some of those happy moments. I was born into the McDonald's family, and I spent a lot of time in the McDonald's world going to work in one capacity or the other from the age of nine years old, and I loved it. By the time I was four or five, dad was a corporate officer out of Southern California. He would take me to his meetings in Westwood just outside of downtown LA and it would be quite a bit of a drive, over an hour to get there and to return home. I would get so excited when I was going to work with him. I would dress up in a pretty dress with my patent leather shoes and my white socks with the ruffles folded over at the ankles. When we were ready, my mom would send us off with a bag of snacks and my coloring books and crayons.

"OK, Kiana don't bother your dad when you get there. If you need help just wait until there's a break and stay quiet so your dad can do his work."

"OK," I would say, and off I went. I truly loved it when I got to go to work with my father.

I remember riding in the big elevator and because dad worked high up, I would love when the elevator ascended and opened into this beautiful workplace where he was the head man—the boss. When I walked into the office with him, I felt so proud. Everyone was so kind, nice, and loving to me. I felt good about myself and enjoyed being in this entirely different world. I would sit in these meetings, and I would listen and watch quietly as people would go in and out of his office. Often I would sit at the conference table coloring, and I especially loved it when dad had me sit in among all his staff. I would stay quiet, and I would listen and watch. I felt so important and grown up.

As I got older dad would tell me on the way to work what the business meeting would be about. When we arrived, I would enter the room and take my seat quietly from where I'd keenly observe the interactions of all the people in the room. On our hour-long journey home, he would ask my thoughts on the meeting and what I had learned. He didn't just want an overview; he would get into the details about my thoughts on the whole conversation. Then we would have another entire dialogue around my takeaways. What he was doing was observing just how I was processing information and helping me expand how I saw the world. It was schooling to understand intentions versus what was being said and, more importantly, what wasn't being said. I'd come to understand, that finding the truth in communication was nuanced by what people were not saying.

Being able to see people for who they are was another important lesson from my dad. Through dad's training, I learned to evaluate people through their lens rather than through mine. And while evaluation or judgments still come, I know I am a better leader because of my discernment ability. Asking questions about how I understood things was his way of assessing me. Dad would give me his opinion and we were able to go back and forth, he always expanded how I thought about things. Those expansion exercises helped me to understand there was more than one way to think about something and that everyone's opinion mattered. It didn't mean everyone was going to get their way, but if you had the heart to listen, the heart to learn, and the heart to bring people together over a common mission, then suddenly real change happens. As a child, McDonald's to me was always a place filled with opportunity. Now I see it as a place filled with opportunities for people willing to choose upward mobility if they they're ready to do the work.

When dad left corporate life and made the move to becoming a franchisee, he had a hard time going from being a man of influence and having the impact to make change, to walking into his two locations to learn how to run the business. Life became a financial struggle and dad was heads down as he focused on running the family business.

Time flies whether you are having fun or not. With high school behind me, I was now faced with a decision about my career and college choice. College was not an option but an expected next step. When I told my basketball coach, I wanted to be an entertainment attorney he actually sat me down and told me, "You'll never get into law school, so you need to redirect your focus." I was hurt. Then I felt this awful shame that I was not intelligent enough to pursue my dream. Devastated, I at once changed my major from English to Business. I was so used to going along to get along that my dream of becoming an entertainment attorney fizzled in the face of public opinion. It was never really a dream like a NorthStar dream because I didn't know who I was to have dreams.

What I didn't know then was, what mattered was what I wanted, and it didn't matter what others thought was good for me, or about me. Uncertain of my choices, it was easy to be swayed by the many people, from my high school counselor to my dad, in my ear telling me what I was capable of or not.

My mom was intent on me getting a basketball scholarship so they wouldn't have to worry about paying for my schooling. I was good enough to have several offers and accepted a scholarship to the University of San Francisco (USF), which had made the sweet sixteen the year before. The USF coaching staff also reminded me of my high school experience and that was a plus.

So, I went to USF on a basketball scholarship. It was no surprise, because recurrent in my life when uncertain, I was prone to being influenced, and I rarely rebutted. The peculiar thing is, if I wanted something, really wanted it, there was no way I would give up until I got it. So, I know I could be relentless, but I never had the spirit to fight for a dream I barely understood. I honestly had no idea in what direction to go. I had no clear path to what I wanted to do for a living. I knew I wanted to dance, but if you'd asked what that meant or represented back then, I would probably have answered, "A dancer is free." I couldn't name the thing I was searching for, but whatever the thing was, it would allow me to express the freedom I sought. So, I left my dream of being an entertainment attorney with my coach. It turns out I haven't regretted it as business is where I shine.

In college, I played on the basketball team for two years and then I got injured. The school allowed me to keep my scholarship and I did things with the team but was benched. There was a wonderful side benefit to this because, like in high school, dad would fly in to see me, take me to lunch, and then fly back home. When the team was at away games, he'd fly me home for the weekend. Midway through my Junior year, I wanted to transfer to anywhere, a local university near home was my preference. I just wanted to go home but my parents could see no value in that since staying put meant I would graduate debt-free.

Naturally, I stayed. Thinking I might go into the hospitality side of business, I did internships at hotels but didn't love it. The things that happened in hotels were mind-boggling and I didn't feel I could help people in that environment.

Romantic connections were challenging for me. I would always keep my head down so I wouldn't have to make eye contact with people. I didn't want them to see how I was living in fear, and to be quite honest I didn't want to see it in myself. It was bad enough that whenever I looked into a mirror I would break down and cry for hours. I got good at avoidance and pretending nothing was wrong as I was super focused on getting the things that needed to be done. In high school, I hadn't dated much, hardly at all. In college, it was an eye-opener that men found me attractive. I wasn't unaware of what I looked like; it was just never a part of my awareness to care about such things at all. Because I had long concluded men really didn't find me attractive, it wasn't until my late thirties that I owned my beauty. So, here I was instead of am in college and for the first time in my life some men were interested in me; and the caveat, many were taller. At first, I often missed the cues of engagement and would respond in ways interpreted as being shy, rude, or aloof. I didn't understand then that my actions, all motivated by fear, were pushing people away.

My girlfriends saw to it that I became a bit more social. I began hanging out in their social group. In the group was this cool guy who was an amazing, fun, easygoing baseball player who just happened to be white. I liked being with him. It was comfortable and I felt safe and I was honestly attracted to him. We began dating, well more like hanging out, and it was wonderful. The best part was he was tall—taller than me, good-looking, and super popular. The worst part: there were a lot of women who liked him and he was white. Not because he was white, but because of what I expected as comments from home. That was not my father's vision for me. Still, I liked hanging out with him, and since it wasn't super serious, I figured it'd be okay.

I told my parents about him and my dad in his loving way was supportive, but true to form then proceeded to squash the idea of me dating, much less marrying a white guy. Unbeknownst to me, dad asked his McDonald's cronies if there was an African American in the group with a son who would be a good candidate for his Kiana. So, they all got together, and as it turned out, one of dad's dear friends had a son who was quite tall, not quite as tall as me, and so they set up an opportunity for us to meet. I liked him. He was a nice guy, but I didn't see him much because I was more infatuated and enamored with my college friend.

Soon after meeting Craig, I was asked by my dad to go to a McDonald's All-American All-Star game, and Craig "happened" to be there as well. That day we hit it off well and so became friends and started talking regularly. Over time we started dating and a few years later I found out the meeting was a setup. My dad and his friends had arranged for me to meet Craig so I wouldn't continue with my crush from college.

Craig and I met when I was a sophomore in college. I was around nineteen. We reconnected when I was twenty and we got engaged when I was a few weeks shy of my twenty-second birthday. His proposal was a bit dramatic for me as I am not one for grandiose celebrations for personal, and private moments. So here we were, sitting in Mel's Diner, and in front of a whole bunch of people, he asked me to marry him. I was both embarrassed and joyful at the same time. I was also a little miffed because I still had this imagery in my mind of what it would have looked like when one gets engaged, more like a romantic movie, and this felt more like a comedic spoof on a rom-com. I was happy someone wanted me as a life partner and it felt really good, but I couldn't fully express my joy with people around me, so not until we got back to my apartment and it was just between the two of us, I got to fully celebrate. With Craig I didn't have to put on a show or feel I needed to self-protect. I could just be with him and that was that.

A few months later my great-grandmother passed away. Even though Momma Annie was my dad's grandmother, he called her Momma because she was his mother in every sense of the word. Dad asked us to postpone our marriage for a year, so he'd have time to mourn his dear grandmother. Craig wanted to get married the summer after I graduated college and when I suggested we wait a year, he felt I was choosing my family over him. That's exactly what I was doing, but I didn't see it that way because I couldn't understand his rush to get married. We were so young. Why couldn't we allow the year of mourning and healing my dad needed? How did he expect my family to mourn someone so dear and plan a wedding for their only daughter at the same time? I felt it would certainly be better to start our life with a clear runway. Craig obviously could not see my logic. Tired of the back-and-forth arguments we were having over my choosing my family over him by asking to take an extra year, I felt he wasn't choosing me or the well-being of my family. I truly couldn't understand the need to rush! A few months after I graduated from college and a few weeks after being home we broke up. It was a very painful breakup for me. I truly thought he just needed time to rethink.

I waited for two years for the day I would see him at another McDonald's convention. I'll never forget seeing him for the first time after our breakup. It was during a McDonald's convention in Las Vegas at an evening celebration where we were attending the National Black McDonald's Owners Association extravaganza. I had dressed to the nines in all white and I knew I was looking good. For over two years I had carried the hope in my heart we would one day reconcile and get back together, but there he was with a woman who had a ring on her finger. In disbelief, I told my dad I thought Craig was engaged. My dad's response was, "Engaged? Kiana, Craig is married." I was devastated beyond belief. Everybody there knew how devastated I was. My mom's friends came and took me and wrapped me up in their arms and said, "Kiana you gotta hold it together. Don't let everyone see your pain." And though I knew how never to let anyone see me sweat, it took quite a few years for me to no longer be a walking ghost. My dream had been shattered and I had no idea what straw to hold onto now.

After my breakup with Craig, I had a temper tantrum for the first time in my life. It was a meltdown, but it also felt good to release real emotions. Still, I decided love was not for me. I became a serial dater. I was never one to have multiple partners at one time, but I would date a guy for about three months, sometimes six, and then end it. I would dump him and then go to the next. It was a craziness of constantly searching for a love to save me when no love could save me. I didn't realize that until I loved myself no love would find me because I was not in a space where I could love anyone back.

With my focus on nothing I had no idea what I wanted to do. My plans to get married and move to the East Coast had fallen flat and I had no other plans, so I returned home with no aspirations in mind. Within days my dad made it super clear, "You have to get a job. You can't just sit around here doing nothing; you have one year to move out." And he was serious.

Three weeks after college, in July, I got a job working for, coincidentally, a chain of tall women's stores. I started as a salesperson and within a few months, I was promoted to store manager. I was good at my job so a few months later I became the assistant buyer. As the assistant buyer, a job I didn't like because it was boring and I was simply shuffling paperwork by myself, my performance started to slip. It just wasn't a fit for me who preferred people interactions. I began to travel around the country to visit the other store locations and went to buying shows, which I liked because I was around people.

In January, right around my birthday, six months after he'd told me I had one year to live at home, my dad handed me a newspaper with places circled in red on a map. On the map was the name of a realtor. "Call him," dad pointed to the card. "Have him help you find a place you can buy—within this radius." The hilarious thing was, that the areas circled in red where he said I could live were geographically close to my parents. He then reminded me, "You have six months out of the year I said you could live here left. Here I am offering you a job that will allow you to move out and support yourself."

"But Dad, I'm not sure what I want to do exactly."

"Exactly. So, here's what I think you should do. Come to McDonald's and become an owner-operator."

Until that moment I had never wanted to work at McDonald's as a career. It was the last thing in the world I wanted to do because I didn't want a life like my parents, but it was an offer I could not refuse. The sweet spot of his offer as I understood it was, that I could become an owner-operator and create the life I envisioned for myself. So, on the first of March the following year I joined McDonald's and went to work for my parents as an assistant manager. Six months later I was a store manager and nine months later, a supervisor.

As we grew in number of stores and things started to settle once again, as an owner-operator dad began to take on leadership roles for owner-operators as per their request, which meant he would again attend national conventions now as a franchisee leader and he would take me to monthly leadership meetings whether they were national or international. I was now sitting in meetings with owner-operators' leadership and corporate officers, CEOs, and CFOs of the global McDonald's chain in the United States. The same traditions would happen. We would drive to the meetings and as before he would give me pointers on the agenda and tell me what outcomes he was hoping for. Dad would talk about the dynamics he wanted to create in the meeting without it being dictatorial because he insisted people offered their best selves when they felt included. While I was with him, Dad would be on and off calls and I'd listen to all the different conversations from people from all walks of life and all around the world calling him to ask for his opinion or his advice. And a lot of times, just like he did with me, he would ask them questions to get a clear understanding before he gave his opinion. That is still dad's directive: listen to what is being said, and more importantly what isn't being said. Only then should I form my own opinion about what happened at a meeting? On the drive home we would talk about it as usual but this time he would ask my advice about what I thought he should do. I never really realized this was such great training until much later when I was in a leadership role. My dad, when I thought about it, really gave me the gift of understanding how to lead through the lens of people being successful together.

I found joy being with my dad and came to realize that just like my dad, I have an uncanny ability to get the best out of people, not by making them compete, but by creating an environment of cooperation and collective problem solving leading to solutions that worked for many, not just for a few. Being a vital part of this kind of team process is where I excelled. It truly is my superpower. The experiences at McDonald's taught me how to work hard, and how to persevere and proved invaluable when I eventually went on to helm our family business.

MCDONALDS: MY ROLE AS CEO

For the next few years, I focused entirely on my work. My ascension to a supervisory position was rapid. I was being trained to take over the company when I discovered the Director of Operations, my dad's right-hand person, was embezzling from us and was dismissed without severe consequences. In fact, he went on to become a McDonald's operator. I was expecting we'd hire someone to replace him, but my dad said, "Well, now it's your job." So, I stepped into the role of Director of Operations and the role of President of our company. I was all of twenty-six, so young, and though I knew I was a problem solver, I had never had this level of responsibility before. I had never run the entire operation and had only been in my role as a supervisor for maybe a year. Though I had been going through a training program with McDonald's for about two years learning all the back-office stuff, which was one of the reasons I was able to catch what was happening, I was hesitant. Unsure I could take on this much responsibility I asked, "Dad, why do you think I can do this? I'm not ready. I'm so young." Dad, with all the confidence in the world simply looked at me and said, "No, you can do this. It's your time."

From a young age, my dad had been grooming me for this moment. Whether it was because this was a role he didn't want to take on again, or he needed someone to step into the position immediately because of his national and global leadership roles; it seemed I was the best choice. Because I had shown proficiency and a willingness to learn, he truly believed in my capabilities to helm the company. I was pretty sure, it was a combination of all those things, and because dad had always seen something in me and would often say, "You're just better at this than I am. You have a skill set I don't have."

He was ready to put his confidence in me. At that moment, I had a glimpse into why God had ordered my steps. It was the first of my illuminations that would come not always as gifts but as stepping stones. As a young child, I had always been "doing" for my family. Why would the present be different? What seemed like an early burden had given me skills now advantageous in my new role. I'm the one who can see the entire picture and I was the family's problem solver. I had the uncanny ability to know at any given moment where to drop in to either fix or change something going stagnant. I instinctively knew when to push us forward and when to shift directions. It's not something I was trained to do on the job per se, it was just how I function in life, from living the life I was handed. I'd been an operator my whole life, and this job was about operating. I have no qualms claiming I'm a phenomenal operator. I know how to operate businesses. I know how to build teams, get resources working for us, how to pull back, and how to move forward even when it seems impossible. I know how to redeploy resources even when they look like they are running out. It's just part of who I am. So, I stepped into my role with a level of confidence and set new goals to reach for the business and my family.

As the President and COO of the company, I was now reporting to my dad. At first, I tried to emulate everything he did, but his style was not mine. As a take-charge person, I can be empathetically pretty bossy. Once I hear all sides of a story, I have no compunction in saying, "Well, this is how we're going to do it," clearly laying out all the steps. True I had false bravado, but I was willing to fake it until I made it, which I knew was just a matter of time. And it worked. When I tried to do things my way dad would change them back to the status quo and it was very frustrating. It took me some time to learn how to work with him now the buffer between us was gone. I was on the line for the results my authority required, and I needed to do things my way and never doubt my ability to do a good job. But my dad and I had to learn how to navigate, and I would be constantly telling him, "Dad, you can't just walk in and make changes. I made those changes on purpose. There's a reason for the things I do."

So used to his authority nothing changed immediately. After about nine months, I finally went to him and said, "Dad, you have got to stop. I am in charge. Let me be in charge. If you believe I can do this, let me do it! If both of us are in charge, there will be chaos and confusion. There can only be one leader—one worker one boss, and you asked me to do it. So let me be me."

To my dad's credit, he did. To my surprise and delight his response was, "I've been waiting for this moment."

Blessed with my problem-solving skills, I had a 360-degree view of an issue and could wrap a solution around it. Doing things, the way I felt they should have been done led to my success in the family's corporation and I began hearing the usual, Kiana will fix it. I was very comfortable with having responsibilities. I wasn't afraid of it. Whatever had to be done, I was going to find a way to figure it out.

When I fully embraced my role and claimed it, it immediately changed how I navigated my new life. The moment I claimed ownership of leadership, I also claimed the responsibilities and accountability for the company and my parents' financial well-being. There was no way I was going to fail. My dad could see I was committed and that freed him from worry. This shifted our relationship yet again and I really started becoming the true boss of our family business. This final shift created this beautiful relationship between Dad and me, and I would go to him when I really needed his help and support or use him as a sounding board because of his wealth of knowledge, experience, and wisdom. I made mistakes along the way, but dad allowed me the experience, not trying to ask me to be him. He always wanted me to be myself. I eventually assumed the role of CEO when my father stepped down. But my father didn't really step down, he stepped up.

My dad was a big deal in the McDonald's corporation. Truly, he was extraordinary, and he was a major leader in the company. He was head of all USA National Operators and Chairman and CEO of the Global Operators Network. He was world-renowned within the McDonald's system, and I mean truly all over the world. I remember when we would attend worldwide conventions. We couldn't move an inch before someone would stop my father for a chat or ask him to help them open doors.

With all departments of the company ultimately under my charge, I set out to make my mark. That meant leading from behind and in front. Leadership sets the tone of the organization and I had always seen the world through different sets of lenses, so creating leadership qualities in everyone who worked with me was a goal. I didn't do this because I wanted to lessen my work but because I truly think every human being is a leader. In my mind, leadership first and foremost was honoring who one was created to be, and secondly, never asking anyone else to be me, but to be themself. I was upfront and transparent with our employees. "Look," I would often say, "I'm not easy to work with until you become yourself. Because I'm going to challenge you to be who you are. And I'm never going to stop asking you to grow. Never. I'm never going to stop asking you to expand to become all who you are. And I'm not going to stop expanding myself. I intend to surround myself with individuals who are interested in life, and who are open to finding their purpose here. I'm not going to evaluate you based upon who I am but who you are. If you are on board with this, let's make more magic happen."

That's a big deal to me. That is leadership. Period, end of story. One of the most important parts of leadership is understanding you're only as good as the people surrounding you. It is often said that the top five people in your life determine your trajectory. Few in numbers, I always surrounded myself with people who wanted to do great things.

CHAPTER FOUR
THE REAL WORLD OUTSIDE THE BUBBLE

IN MY ROOKIE YEARS in the early 2000s I remember the first time I stepped into a USA-wide leadership meeting at McDonald's. The room was chocked full of mostly men, with a sprinkling of women, all older than me. I was happy to speak up and proffer ideas I thought were novel, only to have the men tell me my ideas weren't good enough. I got quiet. It was not like the car ride with dad when I was young. At later meetings, the same thing would happen and at first, I would get quiet, retreat into myself, and to my hotel room crying. I would cry a lot. Then I would wipe my face and go to the next session. I took comfort in the fact that it wasn't just me. All the female operators were experiencing some form of dismissive behavior from the men.

With a few more meetings under my belt, I made a pact with myself that at every meeting, no matter what, I was going to speak up at least twice. And I did, but it took quite a bit of courage. Looking back, it was very courageous of me because vitriol would come back when I disagreed with one of the men. Welcome to the C-suite. My dad would counsel me, "Don't be the first one to speak. Always try to be the last and listen, not just to what people are saying but to the things they aren't."

I got good at listening and realized what I was hearing was unspoken fear. Everyone was holding on tightly to the things they already had because they were afraid to lose them. At that point, our mature business was seeded so I wasn't afraid to lose anything. As I started to accumulate my own wealth, I completely understood why people were afraid to make any decisions or take any risks that would jeopardize their amassed holdings.

Winning is a team effort, being able to see beyond the moment is a gift, and being able to appreciate people for who they are, is, in my opinion, a formula for success. There is so much to learn from differences. Recognizing and tapping into uniqueness and appreciating others' uniqueness creates a beautiful tapestry—it creates community, and it is through community that we find our greatest support. This was another lesson in leadership for me. Through this understanding, we can treat each other as the valuable treasures we are however, to do this we need to revise our perspective, accepting and offering grace instead of judgment the same way we would want it for ourselves.

My father reminded me that when I went into those meetings, I was there to lead in facilitating collaboration, so whatever decisions were made needed to work for the majority. If eighty percent of the operators agreed, it was an indication to move forward. If the only focus was to create wealth or create something that only worked for you, then you're leaving everyone else behind. That was a freeing moment for me.

As I stated, most of the leadership of McDonald's were men. It didn't matter if I was a CEO like them or if I was a female who stood 6'2" with an aura and energy that was slightly intimidating. I can't tell you how many times I got propositioned on company trips. I began curtailing my social interaction to avoid uncomfortable situations and accusations or have my body message interpreted as being available. Because of my history of being molested, I didn't have good boundaries with people so discerning whether a behavior was inappropriate, such as touching the wrong body parts or over-familiar hugs, was challenging. I would just get really tense and shut down. I got to the point where I would show up at meetings, give my input, and leave.

At my core, I wanted individuals on my team who showed up as themselves, not as who I wanted them to be. Inhabiting their own world made them equal in the experience they had, which could benefit me. The thing I love about leading authentic people is that I can see who they are from their soul, not from their fear, and I can see how their fear is stopping them from claiming their true soul calling. Because of my dark history, I give people the benefit of the doubt and I'm sometimes challenged because I don't see the dark side of people at all. I've had people tell me this or that person is not good for you. I have trusted those very people because we've walked enough of this life together, but indeed there are always disappointments and that's reality.

In my leadership role, because of my faith, I leaned on God and asked for guidance. I asked that He ordered my steps in the way I showed up, the way I spoke and interacted, and the way I offered guidance. Because of my invisibility for so long, I knew how important it was for people to inhabit their own lives. The benefit to the organization is huge if people are happily engaged and inhabiting their authentic selves. It is true, we all have fears, get angry, and have days when we are upset. That is just a part of being human. My strategy worked. Our franchises began doing well. I decided to date in earnest.

I was getting tired of serial dating anyway when I met someone who I thought I could spend the rest of my life with. For five and a half years we had this on-again off-again torturous relationship before I was done with having my heart in tatters. I was nearing twenty-seven. I convinced myself I wanted to be married by the time I was thirty. Why? Because I read an article a couple of years back that said African American women were the least desired, and if I wasn't married by the time, I was thirty, the likelihood of me getting married was less than fifteen percent My heartbreak man, for reasons I never understood, didn't feel for me what I felt for him so I embarked on a mission to find someone who would marry me. I also wanted to have children.

Nearing thirty, I was introduced to eHarmony which was a big thing at the time. I had been on Match.com but it was not for me. I didn't enjoy it, but eHarmony felt right to me. I had strict parameters of who I was looking for and I wanted to be matched based upon the things we had in common.

Paul was one of the matches. The thing that drew me to him, was his height at 6' 7", a good five inches taller than me. I could even wear heels! This was phenomenal and we began an exchange online and then via phone. The first time we met in person was at a restaurant called Islands. It was a non-pretentious hamburger spot close enough to my home. If the date turned out to be a bust and I needed someone to come and save me, they could get to me within fifteen minutes. It was also far enough away it wouldn't be convenient for him to follow me if I needed to make a quick escape.

I got there first. I was looking up as I was getting into the booth, and he was coming in. On-time was impressive. As he was walking toward me, I remember saying to myself, "Man this guy is funny-looking." Here is this 6' 7" man with strawberry blonde hair, blue eyes, and whiter than white. I mean he was like super white, not a tan line in sight. The minute he sat down he put me at ease and from there on we laughed until we cried. A lunch that should have lasted for our agreed-upon hour was already in its third hour. I was floored. I mean it was so great because I didn't normally engage that way, and it takes a while for me to warm up to people. Apart from having my shield up, I as a Capricorn am generally reserved. Few people knew the playful side of me, and when it came out, they were genuinely shocked. Sitting there with Paul, I was the one in shock because, with little effort, he'd dialed into my playful side. The banter back and forth made for a sentimental moment.

It was always a good time with Paul. I was constantly laughing, and I could tell my funny, sarcastic jokes didn't offend him in the least.

It was very attractive to be with a confident and educated man; he was an engineer, and the experience was liberating. We began dating in earnest and dated for about seven months when we got pregnant with our son. We'd already been down the road of talking about marriage, so, when we realized, we were going to have a child we both wanted and could afford, we said OK, let's just get married. Paul's and my wavelength at the time meshed perfectly and when he asked me to marry him, I was so pleased. It was delightful when he proposed to me in the living room of my condo. There were candles and flowers, and he paid attention to what was important to me. It was really quite lovely. Soon we announced our engagement to everybody, and I'll never forget his best friend saying, "Are you sure you wanna marry Paul?" At first, I thought he was kidding but then realized he really wasn't kidding. It was a red flag, but you know you're hopeful and I really found myself with a man who was also a friend. My parents were supportive, but as expected did not at first want me to be with Paul. They came to embrace him and treated him well.

In 2007, at age twenty-nine, we would marry and go on to have three children, Jason my oldest, was born in November 2007, Sanai in 2009, and by the time I was thirty-three, my third child Samia, a daughter. When our first son was born, Paul and I were happy. Soon after, within weeks, I began to see things that shut me down. We were so different. His family was boisterous and yelled a lot, in my family a raised voice was such an anomaly that if you even laughed loudly people were upset about it. We were in two different worlds, and I didn't know how to function. His big personality overshadowed mine and as it became more his and his, I became more and more suppressed. It wasn't long before the conflict began.

But Paul came into my life for a reason. He brought out in me something called feelings. Paul would bring me to a boiling point where I experienced emotions I had never allowed to surface before. The ability to express my true feelings. I could yell and scream all I wanted or state a truth I would never publicly say with my parents, my siblings, or anybody at work and get an emotional response. I had never fully expressed myself before because I held myself back, shrinking my intelligence and shrinking my power so others could feel better. My family could logic a topic to death and never were emotions a part of any discussions. It was Paul who made me face how the choices I made to deflect and blame other people were all of my choosing. Such was clearly not my understanding. I thought I was showing love. It was Paul who made me see emotions had a purpose, and to this day I'm so grateful to him for giving me the opportunity to learn how to engage and resolve conflict and still walk comfortably through life with someone.

Eventually, though, I just didn't know how to deal with those emotions. Being uncomfortable was my norm and being uncomfortable was much better than feeling anything at all. I would feel a sense of relief when I detonated but it was temporary. I had no tools to deal with conflict, so to be honest I was even more miserable married. I reverted to suppressing myself—to staying in my comfort zone.

When I found out I was pregnant with my third child, I was in turmoil. I had been unhappy in my marriage for some time. Giving birth to Samia held an important clue to God's plan for me. It turned out I had to have an emergency C-section. When the nurse finally brought her to me and laid her on my breast, a feeling entered my body, and for the first time ever my heart opened. I could feel this warmth and a radiating light between our synchronized hearts. I had never felt so much love for anyone. Right then I knew real love existed. I have to believe my heart remained slightly open, though moments later, it felt like I was back in my "rational" mind and state of detachment.

After Samia's birth, I spent two additional years in the marriage, too afraid to leave. Even though my marriage was at its end, we went to couples therapy and I spent our last year practicing how to show unconditional love for my husband. As I was doing this, another miracle happened. I was teaching myself how to love myself...how to be the love I had so desperately been looking for outside of me. I knew when my husband said to me our last Christmas together, he'd bought everyone a present except me because he didn't think of me; it was the end before my new beginning. I had now become invisible to my husband.

Paul and I separated after six years of marriage. We had an amicable divorce, and I was respectful of our time together. Here ten years later, I still consider him someone who has my back in the case of any emergency. He's one of the first people I would rely on because he's just that guy. If you need him, he will be there. Paul will figure it out and he'll drop everything at a moment's notice to help take care of me and our children. It had been so much fun being with him because to this day he is one of the only people who I can laugh with, argue with, and fight with, and it's crazy because we're not compatible enough to live together on an ongoing basis

Paul was a bastion of honesty and truth in my life, but when we got married, I was still unable to share who I was with someone. The emotional explosion experience he allowed me opened a door for me. I am so grateful to him for our three beautiful children who are incredible human beings and I'm so grateful Paul and I have learned how to co-parent in a way that has made our children more whole. I'm also grateful for our marriage because it was an experience most needed for my journey. There are moments where I still can't stand him, and he'll tell me he can't stand me either and I'm so grateful for him because we've always had honesty in our relationship, and that's incredible.

With mounting responsibilities and the need to be in the winner's seat, I easily slipped back into survival mode, all the time operating from my superpower which was to fix problems. As a highly functioning depressed person, I was still able to get a lot of stuff done. I was running the family business I'd taken over when I was twenty-six, which at its peak had over 1,300 employees. Every day I had two thoughts: I was responsible for my parent's financial well-being so I couldn't fail at this, and please God don't let anyone kill anybody today. I was so married to the business and connected to it by the umbilical cord that four hours after my first child was born, I was on the phone making major decisions.

After the divorce, I had custody of my three kids fifty percent of the time which would eventually morph into full-time. I would go home doggedly tired at the end of the day from handling myriad problems, doing back-end administrative and operational stuff, and interacting with people. All I could do was climb into bed. I just needed to come down and not be in the midst of all 90% of the noise at work. I felt guilty I wasn't present for my children who were very young and impressionable. My beautiful and understanding kids would come to my room, lay on my bed and we would play together. Eventually, I would get up and fix dinner and take care of whatever needed to be taken care of in the house, but everything was a struggle. My body was carrying all the weight of responsibilities and expectations and the fear of being a disappointment. It never dawned on me my children were paying attention to how I was presenting to them in this world.

The weight of my own life was a boulder to carry, and I was collapsing under it. I was running hard; on a short leash; and tethered. My therapist wanted to put me on medication. Of course, I told him no because I was not going to be dependent on anything. Period. My job gave me an entire track field because I was running away from life and specifically running away from my own life. Being busy was the drug I needed. Ever mindful of my family's well-being I soldiered on. As the CEO of Webb Enterprises, I was the nerve center of the company. I ran day-to-day operations, which in addition to taking care of my immediate family, was a lot. Knowing I was responsible for making good decisions to protect the livelihood of 1,300 lives was sometimes a daunting responsibility. But I was a good team player, and honestly, I was good at my job. There was nothing I couldn't do or figure out, and my dad recognized that superpower in me. I believe that's why when he stepped down, he made me the CEO of Webb Family Enterprises.

I ran on a fast treadmill motivated by fears, primarily time, and money. They seemed like the two resources we never had enough of, not enough time to get it all done and not enough money to do all that needed to be done. It was fear based on lack that kept us motivated to accomplish all we had. In our home, they were top of mind for my parents, but these were not our values. In fact, they ran counter to the values my parents imparted which were loyalty, being of service, creating parity for others, devotion to family, loving God, staying together, and making good choices. This created an internal conflict which made me feel anxious and entrapped because the two positions conflicted with each other. The only problem with these values is they are the opposite of how I saw life, and though I adhered to them they created conflict for my soul. So, I felt anxious, stressed, and entrapped. Something was coming apart at the seams. How can time be more important than life? How can more money replace internal lack? Until I recognized my soul's journey, I was caught in a web of illusion that time was of the essence and that I needed to earn more money for my family's well-being. My identity and worth were inextricably tied to these fears as opposed to being happy. With all the running I did I still could not outrun myself. That's because when your soul demands recognition it is relentless.

As an unintentional success chaser, I was driving myself hard. My calendar was triple-booked; my meeting schedules overlapped. In reality, my family had so much on the outside, wealth and all that goes along with it: Respect, adoration, superego identity, indulgence, and worldly brainwashing. The material self gives temporary relief through acquisitions driven by the need for more and more as a validation tool, but it was not my driver. What I wanted more of was time.

Having the responsibility and title of CEO of Webb Family Enterprises, I had many privileges people only dream of, yet I was still in turmoil. As the one who held it all together, I thought I was doing the right thing honoring my parents and helping my family. It was what I knew and what I'd always done, but subconsciously I was terrified of losing my identity. In my family, I used self-sacrifice and self-depletion as a way to shore up "love." All the crutches and recognition that came along with my being the "head of family" were undeniably heady. I had a hard time separating but I knew I had to. On automatic pilot, living more like a robot than a human, I couldn't continue this way. There had to be something more this life had to offer me than emotional eating, shopping, and working myself to the bone. Salsa dancing, which had been pleasurable to me since age twenty-one was losing its joy and the freedom it afforded me. When I decided to step into grace, I felt less pressure to be perfect.

The biggest change was, I slowed down the treadmill and eventually got off it completely. In observation mode, I noted that though I was not less busy, I didn't feel the urgency of making more and more money nor did I notice the passing of time. I began living in the moment which allowed me to see things differently. In this new world, there was no need to be in a state of anger where I was lashing out or blaming people. Physically too, everything about me on the outside changed. I looked younger. My hair was now natural as opposed to coiffed to fit stereotypes. The clothes I wore changed. My daily practice changed. My body felt pleasure and emotions once unreachable. Being in nature just observing the miracles of all life became important to me. Before, I spent most days inside my cocoon avoiding and suppressing my emotions and now, I live outside of my hiding place ninety percent of the time. I am no longer scared to look in the mirror at who I am on the outside or inside, and I no longer shrink from anything, not even my height. Spiritually, I have grown in leaps and bounds. I wake up and instead of having a hit-or-miss morning, I am intentional about spending time with God in prayer and meditation. One-on-one time with my creator makes my daily walk an attempt to reconnect to my Source effortless. I'm not ashamed of it. My communication with "Source" obliterated my need to communicate all my life with others. I felt so free.

But freedom can be scary at times. Sometimes I felt like my expansion was happening so fast, I'd hold back. Expansion and contraction are constants while in transition and I was in conflict. Inner conflict showed up as aches and pains in my body and I had to find ways of releasing these tensions. I shifted my activities to dancing, cooking, and walking. Expansion itself is powerful, quiet, and scary but being present in the moment instead of living in a story I created in my head was the most liberating feeling I have ever felt. Observing these changes gave me a yardstick of the distance I had traveled. One day I needed to cry. I had no explanation why. I reached for something sweet, a cookie, maybe five and I immediately knew it was a crutch for pent-up emotions needing to be released. I gave myself grace. This shift was hard for me and sometimes I'd just allow myself to cry but I no longer had to put a story around the tears. I didn't have to explain it, nor did I feel the need to place blame for my tears on someone else. I could just be with it, in the moment trusting my soul's current. And I was okay with that.

Overcoming the unsettling feelings of expansion and contraction was a huge milestone and I knew I'd arrived when I didn't put my mask back on. It was a sign I had rejected the notion of the people who often told me, "You know, you don't let people see you in this state." That, *never let them see you sweat* notion had played havoc with how I would instinctually release emotion and now it was over. Being able to separate, to see myself through my own eyes allowed me to stay in the eye of the hurricane. Now, when things don't feel good, when I am angry, frustrated, or sorrowful I can experience all those emotions and still be in profound joy and peace. Rudyard Kipling's message in his famous poem "IF" reminds us not to be shaken by anything, for it is in facing the challenges and obstacles that lead to a satisfactory life. The more I accepted all the things that happened to and around me, and learned to detach from outcomes, the more capacity I had for forgiveness. To be at complete peace even in a state of emotional turmoil meant I had to let go and let God.

My journey created a change for my family but not in the way I expected. The unspoken feedback I was getting, things I might have balked at before, I was able to hear with an open heart and mind. As I grew my spiritual muscle, I came to understand I was the one who needed to manage my experience. I was the one responsible for my feelings and perceptions and I was the only one who could do something about it, but the beauty and challenge of family is you'll probably learn a lot about who you are and they about who they are, as they are the ones you spend the most time with. Family requires patience, forgiveness, and a lot of LOVE. I'm grateful for my family: my brothers, parents, relatives, friends, and especially the three human beings I had the privilege of birthing because they show me every day what's possible when you give people the space to be who they are meant to be. In my family I now know that I am loved; that I am not a bother, and that the world I wish to always create is possible, but sometimes I still struggle to make love feel totally real in my heart.

I understood it may take people time to adjust to my new way of being and that no one changes unless they want to. Once I stopped having expectations and focusing on my pain and tendency to judge, so much came into view. I was able to see my family in a completely new light. A large pain body (unresolved accumulated painful life experiences) for me was around my mother. As I came to appreciate individualism, I knew my mother loved me no less than my father loved me. They just presented differently. I was now able to put myself in my mom's shoes, imagining the frustration she felt navigating life with a debilitating disease. While doing everything she could to please her husband and care for her family the best way she could, she had to concede some of her power. It was strategic. Why wasn't I able to see her? Why didn't I understand the pain of her existence from not being able to take care of her family the way she would have liked, or in dealing with disappointments she experienced around my father? Why didn't I see how she gracefully and gratefully navigated her life? Why didn't I see that despite all the challenges she faced, she never lost her faith in God? She never gave up on herself and they were all expressions of her love. Why didn't I see how powerful she was in the choices she made?

My mother was one of those women who loved God, loved, loved, loved God. No matter what she was experiencing, God was always present in her world. She was a strong woman, who even when sidelined by challenges was every bit as responsible for the success of our family and the benefits our lives afforded. Why hadn't I seen that for so long?

I was also able to see my dad's need to move as far away from the life of poverty he'd known. Driven, his life was dedicated to making sure, that even if he fell one or two rungs as he climbed, it would be nowhere near the bottom of where he started. I could see his dedication to parenting because he had had no reliable parent. I could also see the many times he'd disappointed Mom and had no patience for those who did not do as he said.

I could now clearly see my brother Karim's need to distance himself from family so he could find his own path, and I could see why Kyle so desperately needed to move out of my shadow and into his own light. Kyle's lashing out was very painful for me, but it was what I needed to happen to catapult me on my journey and what he needed to figure out who he was outside of me as a parental figure. I knew I had to let him go for both of us. The easiest way to let go when cleaving the parental umbilical cord is to lash out and hurt the one you love. I now understood his frustrations. My love for Kyle has always been and will always be unconditional. I believe he was certain enough of that to take the chance on a painful separation knowing he'd never be abandoned, certainly not by me. Even though the actions he displayed were upsetting and still in some ways triggered me, I have no story to spin.

As much as I was a teacher for Kyle, he was one for me. Amy, his wife, was the glue and one of our guides who saw us through it all. She'd repeatedly ask us to have the hard conversations. Through those conversations, I emotionally came to appreciate I could be in multiple places at the same time, angry, frustrated, and afraid, yet still very much loving the person who was a light in my life and the bane of my existence. I could also now see how I held my family hostage to my pain in one way or the other. I was the beneficiary.

It didn't matter whether my family could immediately adjust to the new Kiana or not, the process had begun. Because we have a common direction, our North Star, so to speak, and we love each other no matter what, we will build something great to pass on to our future generations. Our lack of communication and our inability to share how we truly feel created a space for mistakes to occur, but they too are lessons. The image of our perfect family on the outside was not everything we experienced on the inside, and it was time for us to face that. It was a place I needed to get to.

As a family, we have always been a support for each other, not necessarily in the way each of us needed it, but that we had each other's back was a given. Even today we have not healed as a family, but the foundation for our healing is there. As someone walking the path of enlightened unconditional love for myself it means to love all of me and all there is—parts seen and unseen. My belief that there is perfection in the existence of all there is, creates healing for everyone who recognizes it to be true. Loving bigger allows me to pray deeper, to seed my intentions into becoming reality harder, to stay on purpose, and to allow what is happening to happen without resistance even for my family.

At the point when my calling to examine my life came, there was an invitation presented for me to check in on how I was using the time between my dashes. It was an urge I could not deny. The famous dictum of Socrates that "an unexamined life is not worth living," was true for me. Never questioning life, life's purpose, not wanting to know the truth of one existence or the Why of their existence is nothing but a shallow life not worth living.

I can't say any life is not worth living, but I can say, it takes courage to go beyond a programmed life to get to the essence of who we truly are. In so many ways, love is the equalizing and liberating factor that underlies the courage to discover our true selves; to get to our essence.

During my marriage, my brother Kyle suggested that I go to the Landmark Forum a program he had attended at my father's suggestion. My father had been introduced to the Landmark Forum by a neighbor and determined it could be of value to our family, he'd sent Kyle. The Landmark Forum lasts for three days and an evening. At the evening session, one is asked to invite guests. Kyle invited me as his guest. Because it was Kyle who had asked me, and I'm always a yes for Kyle, I said yes. What I didn't realize then but got to appreciate by the end of my time there, was what a gift it was for him to have asked me to do this. The *Forum,* which uses spiritual principles to bring about permanent shifts in one's quality of life sat well with me.

So, at the age of thirty-three, as a part of acquiring my business muscle, I went through the renowned Landmark Forum training program. An amalgamation of breakthrough methodology and transformative learning, the program takes one through the process of removing the blocks impeding both personal and professional success, and harmony. In this program, I began learning and practicing forgiveness and the tenets of unconditional love. If I could ever find unconditional love in my life, I would have a lot of people to forgive, including myself.

Landmark was built on spiritual principles which dovetailed with my upbringing. Every Sunday, you could find me in church with my grandma and Mother. I have keynoted at spiritual conferences, so my spiritual belief was deeply rooted in the church. With new eyes I was able to be more discerning, though I had always been able, at a visceral level, to feel sincerity.

One day, after my speech when we were on a break, I went outside to refresh. As I stood there, not meaning to eavesdrop but within earshot I observed a man and a woman who definitely knew each other talking. The conversation was about how people in the congregation were gossiping about them and they couldn't imagine how they could claim to be Christians. This went on for about two or three minutes. For the life of them, they could not see they were doing the exact same thing they were accusing others of, so when they looked at me and said, "Don't you agree?" my reply was, "Yeah I agree." I took a deep breath and continued, "But sometimes the truth is painful when we are disconnected from love." I am not sure if they got what I meant but it didn't matter. I just needed to say it out loud, not to hurt anyone but as a reminder, "Love is All." This was another yardstick for me to measure my growth because before I would never have said a word.

But when I need a yardstick to check my growth, I visit my family. Before my awakening journey, every time I would go to see my family, my entire body would seize up and I would always be angry. When I left, I would always feel defeated. The thing is, I love my family and I wanted to feel the full impact of our love for each other, so I began learning how to stand in the power of who I am…the I AM. I could let down my guard and reduce the static (my perception) blocking out love's possibilities. The static blocking my signal was hurt, anger, pain, and self-deprecation. If I could learn to trust the divine's time and the universal laws to act in accordance with my desires, then a shift would occur in my perception and therefore my life and I could find harmony in the family I love.

My mom's faithfulness to Christianity and her daily devotion to prayers set the foundation of my religious understanding. In my teens, I rebelled against the idea of religion. I was angry and disgusted with people claiming to be Christians and not acting like it. I was appalled and sat in judgment at their falsehoods, so I stopped going to church or reading the Bible. Let me be honest here. I didn't do much devotion, to begin with, but now I was completely disconnected from religion. Yet my values growing up, the very ones I learned at home never left me, and of course, my years of private Christian schools gave me a good grasp on religion. Though I did not acknowledge it, it was in me. Back then, I lived as if I knew it all.

Because of my mother's deep roots in religion, in my search, I looked to it as a solution and started going to church again, this time by myself. Unfortunately, my disgust was not assuaged because I found many of the churchgoers still as hypocritical as I had thought in the first place. They stood in judgment of everything, but what I didn't realize was that I too, was standing in judgment. I started to attend my church less often and asked my mom if I could attend her church. Every Sunday I would take both my mom and grandma to Faith Community Church, and I would listen to pastor Jim's Sunday sermons. I now began to understand why his messages had been so impactful to many. Pastor Jim was a teacher first and then a preacher who wanted his congregation to use his messages to come to their own understanding of how biblical texts applied to their lives. He also offered his congregation the freedom to question and investigate further what they were learning through his words. When Pastor Jim preached, I could viscerally feel God's presence or not in the words spoken. Some things would resonate and others I categorically knew were not God-centered for me. I would therefore go back to the source, the Bible, and check my soul's feelings against my brain's feelings to find out if the teachings in question were meant for me, and if not, what was meant for me.

Because of the underlying principles of Christianity, I had been more open to Landmark which forced me to confront my denials. I discovered I carried the belief I was a bother. That I took responsibility for others but never for myself. That in the world I had created, I was always blaming somebody else for all the things I experienced. I also got to a level of healing when I was introduced to the idea that all we experience is meant to be a part of our journey back to self. When I acknowledged the truth about my life and followed the *Landmark–*suggested actions of removing roadblocks to success by checking in with people who engaged conflict in my soul, it allowed me to release pent-up angst and step into the sense of relief that letting go allowed. The awareness I gained from this exercise gave me choices about what to do or not to do, and that was freeing. But most importantly, recognizing the awareness I was creating around the experiences I was having were simply stories, and not necessarily reality, blew my mind. For example, the narrative I was a bother, which prevented me from asking for help was false. No one had ever told me I was a bother. My interpretation and the story I built in my psyche were from my expectations and the meaning I'd placed on someone else's response, which could have had nothing to do with me.

At the beginning of my journey, this was a hard concept to grasp. Let me use another example that may help you better understand the concept. I feel rejected by someone who cringes when I hug them. I automatically assume they don't like me and I am not wanted, which is false and stems from a limiting belief. The real story, if one was privy, is, that hugs for this person might represent fear and trigger something that had nothing to do with you. Instead of placing judgment on the cringe and creating a story, why not just ask ask if that happens, "I noticed you cringed when I gave you a hug, I won't do that again without asking."

Landmark allowed me to open the door to awareness and to identify all the places I was holding myself back because of my limiting beliefs. *Landmark* also allowed me to go on a healing journey with my older brother around our childhood trauma. While I had gone through an internal forgiveness journey for my brother and me, I had never expressed out loud our need to forgive. From this session, I came to understand how forgiveness, like love, has multiple layers. When I spoke to him about our shared traumatic experiences it created a new level of healing. Healing helped me understand who I am today has nothing to do with who I was yesterday and that so much growth and maturity can happen between the dash which represents our lives from birth to death. Our once closeness ripped apart began to mend, and I could see him as brand new.

Before I went to the *Landmark Forum*, I had been seeing a marriage therapist for six months by myself because Paul had stopped going. I began doing this therapeutic work a few months after Sanai my middle child, was born. Therapy helped me to see a larger truth and to see how everyone has a story. I couldn't see myself or my story because the wall I had erected blocked communication both in and out. My journey was to see people for who they are; something I value dearly. That I didn't see myself, was something I did not know. How could I value others and value myself when a wall stood between us?

The hardest lesson to accept from going to Landmark was that I was creating the world I was living in, and if I put my intention into what I wanted to create for myself, then I would be able to shift, with certainty, what was happening and swirling around me. I went to Landmark thinking I was going to get the courage to get divorced but what I got was the courage to find unconditional love for Paul. Landmark helped me see my husband and brother as brand new, and maybe it was possible I could see myself that way too.

Marriage counseling for about a year and a half and going back to church before *Landmark* proved to be helpful in my understanding that my truth was not the only truth. The other person's truth is just as valid and as valuable. Equally important is that two rights don't make a wrong no more than two wrongs make a right. Two sides of a story are important so people can come to see the whole picture, experiencing it in its entirety. Landmark's spiritual principles turned on a light bulb in me and at the center of my life, a seismic shift was occurring.

CHAPTER FIVE

I STOPPED WHEN THE WORLD STOPPED

☥

I N 2019 I HAD THE BLESSED opportunity to go to Egypt to celebrate my younger brother Kyle's wedding. He'd fallen in love with and decided to marry Amy, a first-generation Egyptian American. Kyle and Amy invited friends and family to their spiritual joining in Egypt. Her parents who were born and raised in Egypt but moved here after they got married were delighted. A hundred Americans would meet thirty Egyptians on this trip to go on excursions to Cairo, Luxor, and Aswan. I felt out of my comfort zone in Egypt but could not deny its rich history and culture that was beyond beautiful. Experiencing Egypt through the lens of both foreigners and local Egyptians and seeing its magic for the first time with those who had a renewed appreciation of their country was satisfying. Not only was I experiencing different aspects of the culture and history of this ancient land, but I was also appreciating the wisdom of the people.

Right before we left for Egypt, Paul said he didn't want our kids to go on the trip because they were going to get kidnapped. All I kept thinking was, "Man what an awful way to send me and the kids off to Egypt." I kept insisting what he was saying was not true. Paul was concerned because human trafficking and violence overshadowed Egypt. Egypt's notorious reputation as a transit country for trafficking Eastern European women and children to Israel for sex trade work is legendary. I got his concern but didn't feel it applied to us as our trip was tightly buttoned up. I knew this was the right step for me spiritually. One significant reason why we divorced in the first place was because I was on a journey to find myself and he was not at that point in his life.

Egypt is said to be one of the ten energy vortexes around the world, so I was resolute. Finally, he acquiesced with a stern warning, "Don't let the kids get kidnapped." I was far from concerned. We were going to an organized wedding and there would be lots of protection. Egypt for me was a dream come true and I was ready to trust this consecrated place as a stop on my spiritual journey. What was uncanny was, that Amy reminded me that a year into their relationship, I had predicted Kyle would marry her, and she was going to get married in Egypt.

Unfortunately, I didn't get the chance to fully enjoy myself while there, because as a man thinketh so shall it be! We arrived at the hotel at about 2:00 a.m. Egyptian time. With so many of us checking in it took quite a while. Finally, my daughters and I got on the packed elevator with our luggage. My son, Jason, had gone ahead with my parents who had an extra bed for him there. My youngest, Samia, was six years old. When we got to our floor, I got all the luggage off with Sanai, my middle daughter, but my youngest daughter did not make it out in time before the doors closed.

I kept pushing the elevator button, but it didn't reopen. Frantic, and because of Paul's warning, I went into panic mode. I kept thinking about what he'd said and felt even worse. I was bawling uncontrollably. I kept going up and down the elevator back and forth as I didn't know what to do. I decided to leave my middle daughter Sanai with the luggage in case her sister came back to the floor. Sanai was upset because I left her, and I was upset for leaving her. Finally, I found a porter. I explained what had happened and he offered his help. I also went downstairs to alert everyone to be on the lookout. About thirty, maybe forty minutes later the porter returned and informed me he had found my daughter. And there she was! I just burst into tears all over again. For the rest of the trip, I was in hypervigilant mode and couldn't relax. Talk about being a helicopter mom! This was the last thing I wanted to be, but I was afraid to let the kids out of my sight. Though I was on high alert Egypt could not be ignored. The moment I set foot on the hallowed ground of this holy land I knew there was something special about what could truly be a vortex of spirituality. Egypt was incredible. It was so beautiful and at the same time so stark. There was an energy that could be felt even if one was not very connected to "Source". And there was something there I experienced that was triggering.

Being in the pyramids and looking at all that was created, staring in wonder at how it'd been accomplished, which no one still knows, I could feel the presence of creation. To me, the triangular structures represented fully developed consciousness tuned into their intelligence, bodies, and environment. Further evidence of this harmony was the visceral energy emanating from the hieroglyphics and the tombs, especially in the Valley of the Kings. It was unlike anything I'd ever experienced. I felt grounded for the first time in my life and as best as I could, I tried to connect with the energetic field of something bigger. I have never, ever been fully relaxed in my life, but I remember the tombs as the only places where I was able to surrender and fully relax. The writings on the wall in different colors and the energy surrounding me spoke directly to my soul, bypassing my critical, judgmental, and conscious mind. I had this longing to just sit in the tombs and listen to, and study what history wanted me to understand. I was also sitting in the knowing that my sister and brother had created a trip, which was for me a spiritual experience.

The Monastery of Saint Simon known as the Cave Church built into the womb of a mountain, Mokattam, as I walked through allowed me to relive biblical texts of Jesus and his times. The Christian aspects of Egypt were not lost on me because one of the people of biblical times who had always intrigued me as being misunderstood, was Mary Magdalene, and there she was on the walls of the church. Egypt taught me so much about being a spiritual being. It reminded me how intelligent our ancestral people had to have been to create the intricate design of underground tombs and pyramids, and hieroglyphics as communication and storytelling tools that have been around for thousands and thousands and thousands of years. The carvings on the walls, still vibrant with colors have stood the test of time in all their perfection. These centuries-old sites were a reminder that no matter people's interpretation, or their efforts to manipulate history, the truth of one of the greatest civilizations in history stands as a testament to its greatness beyond the influence of the European or Ottoman Empires.

Egypt opened up my heart to a greater understanding of what was possible for me in the world. That my time on this earth could leave a footprint of my truth and existence was comforting. It was for me, an indicator to move my needle from stagnation to prosperity. I was now appreciating why my brother was the catalyst for my growth. And as if it weren't clear enough, the adage "when the student is ready the teacher will appear" played out right in front of me. My resistance to change was the clue.

Two spiritual leaders were leading the trip. They annoyed me to no end with their setting of intentions and requests. They were talking and speaking in this new way about God, referring to God as Source. Their intention setting was not praying but linking up with the Universe. Then it dawned on me. I was pouting. The real story, I was annoyed. Instead of me and my daughters, Kyle, and Amy being chosen, these people were chosen to play a special role in their wedding. I felt slighted and my daughters were disappointed not to be a part of the ceremony. Every day of the trip we were given a new intention by these leaders. To me, if you're going to give me an intention let the intention seed itself over a period of time. In my vigilant mode, I had enough to deal with just keeping track of my kids much less dealing with intention after intention from people I had no idea who they were and what they represented.

Kelly, a sprite little woman who is now Ama, and her husband, Rudy, who also later changed his name to Santos, were two people who annoyed me to no end. On the last day of our Nile cruise, they came over to me and asked, "Can we sit with you?" Mind you, for the entire trip I had been irritated by their presence and energy and avoided them as much as possible. As they sat down in front of me, I began staring at the woman and had this knowing. I remember thinking "Oh shit," this woman is going to be in my life forever. Immediately, I knew we were going to be dear friends. The familiarity that I had known her for a long time was overwhelming. My teachers had arrived and this began my journey into self.

One other gift to me on the trip was my appreciation of the harmony of the people who'd come from different parts of the world and had completely different backgrounds and upbringings, yet were the same. And it was just really lovely. We were able to create a camaraderie and a connectedness that probably would never have happened, were we not there for a common reason, Kyle, and Amy's wedding.

I could feel the shift in my consciousness a month after coming home from Egypt. So, even in hypervigilant mode, there was no denying Egypt was an automatic activator for me. Much of its impact I didn't realize until after I came home. The thing is, I truly am a gift to the world but to find the gem in me, I would need to unwrap a gift mired in guilt, shame, judgment, and fear. If I could strive to find the presence of God and believe and trust God to order my steps, my joy would not be far behind. So, intrigued by the place itself, when I came home, I binge-watched documentaries of this miraculous time in history.

We'd returned from Egypt in November and by December, people were getting sick with COVID-19 and by March, we were quarantined. Like the entire world, COVID-19 put us on pause. There were no distractions to keep up pretenses or bury angst as none of our businesses were operational. The world I had lived in had never seen anything like this pandemic and we had no idea how to cope with it. The isolation, which was a true challenge for many, was not overly challenging for me. I had long been used to being alone. Still, the deaths all around, the rising panic, the fear, and the political warmongering were debilitating to the best of us. With the realization of how fragile life could be, the need to find me took on a new level of urgency. For me, my cohort group was a lifesaver.

Before I went to Egypt, the amazing therapist with whom I had been doing traumatic work passed away. I missed him but had no desire to replace him. As a result of my trip to Egypt and the group of people I met while there, I spent months in a healing cohort. Upon our return, my sister-in-law Amy asked me to go on this eight-week spiritual cohort with her. I did not spend time investigating the group as it was Amy who had asked me. It turned out that Kelly, now Ama, along with her husband Rudy were leading this cohort along with her co-coach Alice. Alice was a longtime collaborator with Kelly on their own spiritual walks and helping other women find their path back to Source. I began the journey of self-healing with Ama and Alice. I had so many questions about where to go from where I was. I was an emotional wreck. Kelly and her dear friend Alice proved to be heaven-sent. I would go on to spend two and a half years on a beautiful journey of self-discovery with them. My first foray into the cohort was an eight-week program called the *Radiant Reboot*. The program included nutrition, Kundalini yoga, essential oils therapy, breathwork, and journaling. But its primary focus was to take the eight women in the group through eight modules of healing to get to a baseline of understanding about our radiance and where it lies. I have to admit I only signed up because Amy said we would do it together. Before the program started Amy dropped out so I was in the cohort by myself, and because I hate to disappoint people and was overrun with being responsible, I stayed. I'd already committed, and God apparently wanted me to be there by myself.

Being in this group showed me therapy had been great for me, but its season had passed. I needed something different to move me toward the fullness of who I was to become. In what I imagined my role would be, I got my next few glimpses into God's ordered steps. Full acceptance of all of me was like reaching nirvana. Almost. And then my brother Kyle would fling open the door to my soul.

I'm far from being a social butterfly so staying with a group of people I didn't know was uncomfortable. I didn't even know Ama or Alice well, so it was very challenging for me. For the first three weeks, I wasn't interested in doing the homework or following the nutrition guide. I would become judgmental about my reason for being there because all of the women there seemed to have so much more significant trauma than me. But like many of them, I was sexually molested as a child and as they were talking about how it had devastated them, I found myself thinking *well blankety, blankety, blank get over it like I did.* I got over it and it's not stopping me from having healthy relationships or getting my work done. What a lie. What healthy relationships? When they cried, I'd be like why are they crying? When they were angry, I'd be like what is there to be angry about? I was in such deep denial. To that point, I had spent my entire life in depression. I was resistant to the notion that the reason was because I had not accepted my trauma and had not truly moved on. People would talk about problems with their parents, and I was like, "Man, I get along great with my parents. I'm not being stunted from having healthy relationships". The truth is I was as dysfunctional as the next. Every single time somebody said something I would at once go into self-defense and self-protection mode. I would fling around statements like, "Well that's not me, that's not me, that's not me at all." I even stunned myself with my own judgment.

As these false statements were falling from my lips, I suddenly realized my limiting beliefs could derail my journey. By week six I started doing the homework. One of the assignments from the first three weeks was to go hug a tree. Of course, my response was that I am not a freaking tree hugger. Finally, I decided to go out and try to hug a tree. I couldn't hug the tree. I then put my hands on the tree, and I suddenly started bawling. I could feel its energy emanating and it was something I'd never experienced before in my life up to that point. How does a child get to be forty and not know the magic of a tree? I just couldn't go back and hug the tree for the life of me because in my head I wasn't enough to hug a tree!

After that day I started paying attention to the stories the women told. Every one of those women's stories was my story. Theirs might have been ten times worse, but like them, I was passing through life as a spectator of my own life. I wasn't living at all. I had been so good at suppressing my feelings and my emotions as the walking dead, that I couldn't relate to their stories. One day, over Zoom Kelly said to me, "Kiana, I just want you to scream into a pillow in front of everybody. Grab your pillow and scream."

I couldn't scream.

She then said, "So, that's going to be your homework for the week. Scream for thirty seconds."

I did it but my throat hurt so badly, I said, well I'm not doing this again. I had no access to any feeling or any emotion. Every single time a new assignment came up I would find myself lowering my defense, though not all the way down. It was a struggle because my guardrails were so welded into the fabric of my being. The more I engaged, talked, and did the homework, the more I felt connected. I started with the nutrition program. I also started tracking when I would at once shut down and return to the walking-dead person I'd become.

Those eight weeks led to the next six-month class, and I loved the class. I was so happy there I was afraid to go back into the world because I didn't want to go backward. My next move was to find a life coach who could help me integrate my past into the vision I had for my future which was coming into view. Coincidentally, Alice the woman leading these women's groups was also a life coach so I spent another six months with her getting personal life coaching as well as going through a support group of women in the cohort. In Alice's trauma coaching experience, I could be part of a group, or I could do one-on-one sessions with her. I chose to have a hybrid where I had my one-on-one sessions with her every week and then I would have two sessions a month with the group.

What was beautiful about this group was I didn't have to hide who I was. More Talk Therapy, I had to talk and reflect. I was beginning to be able to shine my light and be unafraid of unfolding and flowering into who I could become. I could rewind the tape of my existence, and trace back the pain and the loving fingerprints my parents and grandmother imprinted on my life. I realized I had reasons to be happy. I was truly a gift to the world, and I had talents I was ready to find.

I spent time in somatic healing and continued my Kundalini yoga and nutrition program. Through journaling, I found the beauty of reflections. By using my non-dominant hand to write, all my untapped emotions could come pouring out uninterrupted by rational thought. I filled fifteen journals, ninety percent of which were written in my non-dominant handwriting. In those journals, I would ask myself questions and then I would allow the creative side of my brain, which I call the God side, to take the lead. It's the "primitive" part of the brain, not encumbered by logic or reason. Leaning into my emotional brain to answer the questions so much came out about why I was afraid; why I didn't give myself the space to have real intimacy and relationships; and the reasons for all the guardrails I had erected. While this exercise didn't unlock the light in me, it did ease the pressure I always put on myself to do or say the right thing; to follow what my parents asked me to do, and it unlocked the pressure of feeling like I had to be perfect. Regrettably, it didn't eliminate my need to be responsible for everybody else. That came later. For what those six months unlocked, I am forever grateful.

My time with Alice showed me there was so much more to learn. For people to see you, you need to first see yourself. I spent the next year of my journey with her. The first session was a group session and the second was just me and her together allowing myself to be seen for the first time. By allowing me to see myself, I came to appreciate wisdom was already a part of who I AM. It was a very painful experience to face the fact that all these years I had left behind so much untapped potential. What could I have accomplished had I seen myself for all my lived years?

Two years had now passed since I'd been to Egypt and the world was still weathering COVID-19. In the spring, I was invited to a three-day women's retreat designed to help people get in touch with themselves. It introduced me to the possibility of healing with plant medicine. Over the past two years, I thought I'd made strides, but my resistance came up so strongly. I thought, yeah, that's not for me. Since I had been going through a healing journey every time I felt resistance, I learned to ask myself why I was resisting. Resistance became an indicator that helped me find my blockages and where I was not leading with love. Resistance is different from being clear on something you just won't do. Now, if I don't want to do something there is no resistance, I am simply making a choice and I am at peace. When I'm resisting there is a feeling of being out of my comfort zone. It comes from not trusting, from not placing the love from God in my experience.

In addition to all the usual therapies I'd gone through, this group's main focus was plant medicine healing ceremonies and intention setting. I was in prayer about overriding my resistance to this next step as I had never done any recreational drug in my life and outside of college, I had barely drunk alcohol. I was scared about being out of control and I didn't want to be dependent on anybody for my safety. Concerned, I spoke with the group leaders. "I don't even know if I want to do this, but I'm committed to going to the retreat and I'm committed to discovering who I am."

"You don't have to choose right away but we're happy you want to participate."

The workshop leaders were able to put me at ease when they said I could make the choice for me once I got there. Two days before the group started, I said yes to the retreat. For some unexplained reason, I was prompted in one of my non-dominant handwriting journals to read the book of Genesis. I followed the directive and started the readings. I hadn't finished until right before we walked into the first ceremony. I had never before read any chapter in the Bible from beginning to end so I figured it was an interesting prompt and practicing nonresistance,

I had complied. What was interesting to me was I had always been fascinated with why men devalued women. I could clearly see patriarchy in Genesis when we were only a rib and were blamed for temptation. Then I became curious about why Jesus' disciples continually said Jesus loved Mary Magdalene more than anyone when she was depicted as someone who was of lesser morality. Did I feel a kinship with her because of my defilement? I found myself going off on a tangent about the whys of Mary Magdalene, who thank goodness, has been identified as a valued member of Jesus' disciples. These were the things I was mulling over as I entered the ceremony.

There were two leaders for the group session. They were a married couple. The first thing they did was to go around the room and have everyone set their intentions. Out of nowhere for no rhyme or reason, I said, "I intend to know what Mary Magdalene knew because I'm certain Jesus told her something we have no idea about." In a lesser group, they might have carted me off in a straitjacket, but in this group, it was as if I was asking for ice cream.

I was given some herbs. I can't tell you exactly what was given to me, but they were hallucinogenic. The one thing I do remember was, I was given the opportunity to consume an ayahuasca psilocybin blended in chocolate. The herb causes altered states of consciousness often known as "psychedelic experiences." The mixture also included psilocybin, a magic mushroom used by Native Americans for spiritual connection. Like magic, I could feel the nerves in my brain firing. My head was itchy, a little bit painful but I was so grateful because I knew my connections were coming alive, a state my brain had not been in for years.

As I was sitting with the medicine for the first time and my brain was firing away, I felt connected to my body which was shaking uncontrollably. My body was radiating pure pleasure. I didn't realize my body could have sensations at all. I felt myself opening up to all of what God's love is. I felt my body sometimes more, sometimes less, both at the same time. I'd had a similar feeling when my daughter was born; the synchronicity of my being opening up to love, not just my heart but my whole body. Here I was again in a state of pure pleasure, sitting in bliss as my body shook. I journeyed back through the hieroglyphics I remembered seeing in Egypt, but this time I instinctively knew what they were saying to my soul even though I still couldn't read the language. I got the message; I was the reason holding back love. I didn't want to accept that, but it was such a beautiful experience and it helped me to understand how small I had been living and how afraid I was to be big.

I spent three to four hours just shaking. Shaking I was told was my body's way of releasing trauma, releasing the stored-up negative energy in my body, and unlocking the deep level of intuition and wisdom that has always been a part of me. All the energy being released was my body eliminating disease which would eventually have caused sickness and illness.

I've never really felt the need to cry or laugh or scream. I never felt real anger. I wasn't feeling anything. I was walking numb. And here I was in this beautiful colorful state of awareness where my brain, under the influence of plant medicine began to unlock my emotions. And I was so grateful, but also so very overwhelmed. For most of my life, almost forty years then, I had no real association with what feelings meant. When I came out of the ceremony, I was in a state of what I thought was joy. But soon realized it was just a relief I wasn't a walking dead.

One thing I hadn't shared with the group was I'd had COVID-19 during its rage. Though I didn't think it was severe, I was having residual effects—Long Haulers Syndrome. I was beginning to lose my memory and had moments of extreme fatigue. I would be in the grocery store shopping, feeling fine, and out of nowhere, I would be so exhausted I'd have to sit on the floor to get enough energy to finish shopping or to put my cart aside and get in my car and go home. When I got the disease, my symptoms were mild so I didn't see a doctor. With good self-care, I felt my body's defenses to heal would happen on its own. At the point of lost memory and extreme fatigue, I knew I was going to need help. I was ready to get help, but at that point even getting a doctor's appointment proved difficult. That my brain was firing away was such a relief.

Tuning in to love meant knowing myself and opening the door to pain, facing it head-on, and unearthing the hurt around my abuse, family, and the idea of what I thought my family was, which was not all true. Facing reality, a lot of what I believed wasn't about me, but about what my family needed from me from the time I was a mere child, and me, never asking well what about me? What about what I needed? Then I had to face another reality: nobody had asked me to do the things I felt burdened by, not at all. Not my parents, not my brothers. I was the one who took on the role because I was good at it, but more importantly, it brought me recognition. The more accolades, the more I kept doing, expanding my doing into being of service to everyone. Because I was really good at figuring out how to make things work—really excellent— if I say so myself, creating a way when there seemed to be no way, when things seemed impossible, I kept piling on more doing, even when my bandwidth had shrunken to zero. Realizing my "put upon-ness" was of my own doing was annoying and hard to digest.

This second ceremony stripped away any pretenses I had and opened a floodgate of pain and disappointment. The beautiful thing this ceremony unveiled, besides underscoring that my choices were mine, was identifying that my gift would be the stepping stone to reclaiming my joy. Wedded to never asking or allowing myself to feel good in my own skin, I just didn't realize this before. Looking at my life through the wrong lenses was an illusion, the truth was, I hadn't given up anything, I was simply on a journey to discovering myself.

CHAPTER SIX
WHEELS OF CHANGE

☥

THE DECISION TO SELL THE McDonald's part of our business came during this period of my growth. Restructuring our assets, my father appointed me CEO of all Web Enterprises. This caused friction with my brother Kyle. The free fall I went into after Kyle's declaration became the final straw that fully opened me up to the next steps in my healing. What was beautiful about this was I didn't have to hide who I was; I was able to really shine my light and be unafraid of unfolding in the flowering of who I was. My pushback on Kyle's idea of a move forward brought my voice to the surface, something no one expected. After all, I am a woman.

So here is the surprise, one I already knew but refused to acknowledge; I was holding back many of the gifts I'd been given because as a woman I was afraid to outshine others. I was then reminded of Marianne Williamson's quote that became a go-to popular quote by Nelson Mandela: "Our deepest fear is not that we are inadequate. Our deepest fear is that we are powerful beyond measure. It is our light, not our darkness, that most frightens us. We ask ourselves, who am I to be brilliant, gorgeous, talented, and fabulous? Actually, who are you not to be? You are a child of God. You playing small doesn't serve the world." I got it. I have reasons to be happy—I was a gift to the world, and I had talents I was ready to find.

Seeing myself through the eyes of other women and seeing the women through my eyes helped me realize we were all doing exactly that—playing small. All of us were holding back our power within, afraid of being rejected or being criticized. As the womb of life, feminine energy is powerful enough to change the world. Through time it has been subordinated to patriarchy. What often happens, especially for women whose power and influence become greater than expected, and if what they bring to the table is revolutionary, is they are put in their place: husbands cheat; bosses overlook them for promotion; society puts them in boxes of gender roles; enviable people gaslight them, all insinuating they are an intrusion in the life of others, rather than life givers and a gift to the world.

Looking at myself as a gift shifted my entire perspective and some of my fears lessened. My journey so far has allowed me to learn about myself in myriad ways. I was not a detriment to the world, but a gift, and I was determined to focus on healing my body, mind, and spirit to claim that gift, but I needed to find my next steps. I had to put one foot in front of the other and step out on faith. The supportive women's community where I wasn't judged buoyed me. From traveling to Africa, I also began to understand the way forward is the way back through. I had come from an unrelenting ancestry. When I compared my burdens to my ancestors, people who had suffered unimaginable trauma, I began to appreciate how privileged I was because of them. The battles they fought, the sacrifices they made, the terrors they lived through, all in the name of seeking to order their steps toward freedom was akin to my search for freedom. They never gave up and neither would I. There is no comparison between my ancestors' struggles and mine, but knowing I carried the baton of a race of people disenfranchised for so long and the generational trauma I inherited made me embrace resilience. I wanted to find a way to move forward, to honor them, and that could only happen if I honored myself. With my group of women, I reached another level of awareness. Things started unfolding for me which led me to my next step.

On this spiritual walk, I'd embraced, my initial intention was to understand where I stood in my faith. My faith was grounded in religion itself, specifically Christianity, the underpinning of my family's belief. Even then I always struggled with knowing God only through the lens of Christianity. God always seemed bigger to me. It was we humans who made God small. I would go in and out of attending church because I couldn't live with the idea that God was a limited source. I was told my viewpoints were wrong by the good people of the church, nuns at my school, and members of my family. God for me is beyond religion, beyond doctrine, beyond human beings viewpoint; is omnipresent and omnipotent and cannot be contained in one way of believing. On my path, I found out so much, coming face-to-face with the I AM.

There was another healing cohort starting two weeks after my women's group ended. This one wasn't just for women; it was for couples—a Couples Retreat. My brother and my sister-in-law decided to go. Since I was single, I could not attend. As though the Universe understood my needs, the week before the class started Ama called to tell me there was an extra spot and would I like to join the group. I was hesitant as I didn't think Kyle would have wanted me there. Plus, I wasn't married and that would feel awkward.

I spoke to Kyle and Amy about how they would feel if I joined the group. Amy said yes and Kyle didn't say no, so I chose to join the healing circle. Having found some bliss, I wanted to unlock a new level of understanding about what it means to love myself. Still, I was apprehensive, I corralled my fears and took the opportunity to again engage in plant medicine therapy within the group. As I was setting my intention, one of the things Kyle had asked of me, to let him go, came up front and center. I hadn't realized I was holding on to him. Being responsible for him practically my whole life meant I was indeed holding on to Kyle. After our time together on this journey, I looked at him and I looked at myself. It was time to let him go.

This class opened the door wide enough for me to look at all of our lives, my mother's, father's, brothers, and mine. My whole life was spent holding on to something. It wasn't my family per se but the security and the safety they represented. Looking back, I was able to see my family was not the family I had stored in my head. Life was not all roses. I had protected with my silence my father's infidelity, my brother's rebellion, my mother's acquiescence. Being a child responsible for my family, my entire self-worth had been tied to how much my family needed me—my listening ears for my mother's disappointments; my stellar performance to sustain my father's success; my motherhood for Kyle. How much more could I give? Was the only reason for my existence to be of service to them?

Kyle needed to break a bond. It was important for him, and I needed the family to see me for who I was and affirm my value and my worth as the nucleus of the family. I needed to see my family for who they were as individuals and I needed to see me. Once I understood people only see what they could see from their perspective and most didn't see the full picture, a missing part of my puzzle fell into place. It was denial that was causing our logic-ing responses in the first place.

There were times I felt slighted when some of the credit I thought belonged to me was given to my father. Yet, what should it have mattered? Why did my ego need those accolades when our family's journey together represented a collective effort for our success? I didn't need to be seen by anyone as long as I could see myself. Understanding who I AM in God, once I stopped trying to be seen or valued by others, took me to a level of peace and freedom.

There is a valuable lesson to be learned for all of us. Every time someone says you are holding them back, the reality is you're not the one holding them back, you are the excuse. And every time you feel held back, you're using it as an excuse for holding yourself hostage. What I needed to do now was let go of the idea I needed to hold on to anything, including Kyle. Free from the expectations and desires of finding love from someone, something, or somewhere outside of me, I settled into a new groove. For me to move forward, I now needed to understand who God is and what God's love is or isn't. This I would learn on my next journey.

Brothers and Business

My brother's name Karim Malik means generous king and he's lived up to his name in my eyes. I was close to Karim as a child. My mother tells the story of me running after him and him being so generous and gentle with me. Mom said he adored me and looked out for me. Being four years older than me he was shifting into teenagerhood when I was still a child.

By the time Karim was in sixth grade, my mom would say he had an affinity for girls. She would say it with disdain, no doubt triggered by her experience with her dad's and my father's wandering eyes. I knew then Karim's experience with my family was different from mine and as the first-born child, my dad's expectations for him were hard to live up to. Additionally, Karim was a trigger for dad who espoused family loyalty yet was himself challenged to fulfill his vows to mom. Though dad strayed he stayed with our family but in turn, it created dynamics that affected us as kids as the rift between mom and dad deepened and lasted nearly eighteen months. The mixed messages we were getting were not something to face but to sweep under the rug.

As dad and Karim's conflict escalated, Karim retreated from the home. By the time he was twelve, he'd spend most of his free time with his friends, so I saw him less and less. Mom did her best to protect him, but in solidarity did not overpower dad's decisions as her role was to keep us in line. So, Karim always felt unprotected in our family. Heavy into Gangsta rap, Karim found himself in the wrong crowd and was headed down a slippery slope. Always outplaced, which was clear when Kyle was born and Mom moved him out of his room of twelve years to the guest bedroom to make room for Kyle, which made him rebel even more. This so hurt Karim, there was no hope of repairing the damage done. He sought refuge and funneled his anger into his rebellion. Seeing him as disobedient, my father was even harder on him, even putting him out of our family home. Despite all this, he was very much a part of our family business since the age of nine, rising in the ranks from handling the grill to manager and approved owner. College-age, Karim went off to Morehouse but two years later was back home. At twenty-three he married, had a child, and moved away to the Virginia area to work with McDonald's corporate. He returned to the business when his marriage ended, but unable to work with dad he struck out on his own and became successful in his own right. I admired how brave he was to step out on his own and create a full and meaningful life outside of the family and the family business. As part owner of several Buffalo Wild Wings franchises, he is the child most independent of the family. Somewhere, somehow, he was listening to his own drum.

My mom really wanted Kyle, the baby of the family, to be born on my great-grandmother's birthday, but he came one day later. Kyle, unlike Karim and I, never experienced the struggle of expansion and contraction of our wealth as dad moved from Corporate to franchisee. Kyle could not have been cuter and I doted on him. So many times, he was the light in my darkness, and I assumed responsibility for Kyle as soon as he was born. Due to my mom's MS flare-up and being bedridden, I became Kyle's de-facto mother and he'd call me mom to the chagrin of our mother.

After high school Kyle moved to Atlanta to attend Morehouse and then worked with Disney. Our franchises were doing well, and I was really in need of help. My children were young, one just born, and I needed someone I could trust to help me, so I recruited Kyle from Disney. I gave him an offer he could not refuse, much like dad had given to me.

In 2010 Kyle came to our company as the CFO and owner trainee. To help his position, he furthered his education earning an MBA at

USC and at Wharton. We were polar opposites in the way we processed things, and it was a wonderful experience for me to partner with Kyle. I felt we were finally going to experience life as equals and while I was his boss and older sister, we would share the responsibility of caring for our parents' financial well-being. For the first time in my life, I felt like I had someone who truly had my back as I had his. Kyle and I were able to talk about our business, the fears we had, our hopes and dreams and he helped me make sense of my marriage and offered support.

Now able to spend more time with my children I was experiencing a whole new lifestyle. I had built up enough reserves and had access to a large enough equity line of credit so no matter what McDonald's might ask us to do in the future, we would be able to meet it and exceed it and that gave me comfort as I relinquished some of my control.

Around this time, Karim presented dad with a proposal to invest in a fine dining establishment in the Inland Empire. I was adamantly against this and told my dad no way should we do it. I was especially emphatic that if anything should go wrong with the restaurants if we made this investment, we would be cash-strapped. But dad, feeling some guilt around his and Karim's relationship, decided to invest. I owned three of the seventeen restaurants at the time and reminded him it was his money so if he wanted to move forward, I would support him, and we'd figure it out because that's what I do. In under two years, the restaurant had to close. In ways I cannot explain I began to feel things were beginning to break down. By 2016, I was feeling the constraints McDonald's placed on my life. I began discussing with my family, but especially Kyle my need for growth and what I needed that could no longer be fulfilled at McDonald's. I had no room to expand or explore and I had too much responsibility.

I had always seen the world so differently and as much as I loved it at McDonald's, I had outgrown what it had to offer me. McDonald's however tightened the pressure in the cocoon I held myself in because I was too afraid to leave, to go out on my own, to disappoint or abandon my family, and to give up the security it represented in my life. I pushed down my desire to abdicate to keep the comfort of my surroundings, but the truth is I was miserable.

I look back now at this feeling of misery from my self-sacrifice, and I sit in profound gratitude because I never, ever want to return to this place of ever rejecting myself again. I knew in my heart there was something out there for me bigger than what I was experiencing. I would find it, no matter what. For the next three years, yearning and longing for some level of freedom, I soldiered on juggling my life and my mental state. Taking care of my family, and children, and the business was grueling. I was traveling quite a bit during this time back and forth from Los Angeles to Chicago every three to six weeks to attend meetings and conferences for the McDonald's diversity groups I represented. In addition to all my superwoman and super-executive duties, at the time I was still in the process of separating and ultimately divorcing my husband.

In 2020, when COVID-19 hit, my forced short-lived hiatus was soon gone. After our initial shutdown, the government decided food was an essential need so our restaurants reopened. Business wise it was the most challenging time I have ever experienced. For the first few months, it was hard to surmount the challenges of the business, but it was even harder to deal with the grief, loss, and uncertainty our employees and our community faced.

One of the benefits of the shutdown was the habit of walking five to six miles with my sister-in-law Amy, five to six days a week. It gave me time to think. With time on my hands, I was forced to face the grumblings of my psyche. Amy was God sent. I found myself able to talk and share with her some of what was truly on my heart.

My parents transitioned their business assets to Kyle but I held the majority shares. My interest in the business had been waning and selling was on my mind since 2016. As we were always seeking ways to diversify our family business, every year-end, Kyle, and I would assess the state of the business with our trusted advisors to ascertain the best moves for our family. In November 2020, our accountant said if there was ever a meaningful time to sell it was then. I looked at Kyle and he looked at me and we both knew we were ready to sell. We called a board meeting with the rest of the family and presented the opportunity. We all came to a consensus. I, being responsible for my parents' financial well-being felt it was time for them to have the payday that would set them up for life, and that went for everyone else as well. Kyle had been in the business for over ten years and Karim had re-cemented his relationship and was back in the fold so to speak. God was in this mix so however I pivoted I already knew I was going to create even more wealth for my family.

Immediately, I went into action reaching out to people in our circle to see if they had an interest in purchasing our business. One was the previous director of operations I had brought in a few years after I'd joined the company, who had himself become an owner-operator and agreed to buy eight of the stores, and another in our circle the others.

During the assessment period, while McDonald's reviewed the deals, I told Kyle and my parents I wanted to take a break before we firmed up any decision on our next business move. When we sold the first eight McDonald's there was a month between the next closing, but Kyle and my parents insisted we move towards a decision now. I was insistent, not ready, and if they wanted to move forward without me, I was okay with that. It seemed to me after all these years of hard work, we could take a moment to enjoy the fruits of our labors, each other, rest, travel, and experience life on a different plane before reconvening our next business steps as a family. I wanted us to come up with options as a family that left no one out.

It was an honor to know I was successful in my role as CEO and that was clear in the sales number the businesses commanded. The outcome: everyone ended up with a great net worth. Had the pandemic not happened we would probably have waited the additional twenty years our exit plan called for. This early sale gave us each an opportunity to look outwards to our business interests close to our hearts and for the family to diversify our portfolio into other areas. A great deal of the credit for our success, and rightly so, was given to my dad. Financially, over and above the shares he owned, Kyle and I honored my parents financially. Acknowledged or not, I knew my contribution was felt and it added a few zeros to everyone's personal wealth. With the sale behind us, everyone was searching for the next move for the family unit except me. I never questioned the fact that as a family we would achieve great things again, but I also wanted us, as individuals, to do the same. I was ready to move on. I wanted to create a world where people were living in their glory, creating lives of fulfillment as opposed to living in fear they didn't want. I could feel it. The call was clarion.

CHAPTER SEVEN
THE AFFRONT
FEELING DECIMATED

☥

MY WHOLE LIFE, UNTIL KYLE'S statement took me by surprise, had been dedicated to the well-being of my family. When I took the helm of McDonald's, we had twelve stores. As dad had suggested when I was approved as an owner-operator, I was able to buy two more stores on my own and bought three additional locations bringing our store total to seventeen. When Kyle joined the company after completing his McDonald's owner training requirements, he was awarded a percentage of the stores dad owned. Under my stewardship as CEO, the stores flourished and even those in the red had grown to become profitable. With a desire to diversify in 2007, at the suggestion of Kyle who had valuable input as a family steward, the family created Webb Investments—a holding company for shared assets allowing us to diversify investments for the family. It was separate from Webb Family Enterprises, the company managing the operations of all the McDonald's stores. It was its own entity but fell under my auspices as I was the CEO of Web Family Enterprise. As I normally did, I took it under advisement.

While I was still processing the idea, a habit of mine is processing out loud, Kyle acted and implemented the plan of creating Webb Investments and the opportunity to subordinate Webb Enterprises under Webb Investment. Kyle would then assume the position of CEO of Webb Investments when he joined the company in 2010. Webb Investments at the time had invested in seven diverse companies from technology to cold storage and some real estate. I had been remiss in not noting this move back them, but nothing had changed as I continued as the CEO of Webb Family Enterprises, the seventeen stores and Kyle reported to me. In 2021 we inked deals in March and April to sell our McDonald's franchises. Kyle wanted to do real estate and I wanted to create something that was my own, something that came from me.

In 2018 my had dad become very ill. He wanted to leave a legacy when he was spared from the brink of death, so he created a company called CEEM (Cooperative Economic Empowerment Movement). Dad brought his vision to us and asked Kyle and I to help him get it off the ground. I knew I could not helm the company as I had my hands full with McDonald's. I asked Kyle if he wanted to take over as the CEO of McDonald's or if he wanted to helm CEEM. Since Webb Investment was in its growth stage and waiting on our next move, Kyle honored our dad's dream of giving back to his community and chose to become the CEO of CEEM—a membership company created to invest in Black-owned businesses with the ability to scale. The goal was to bring on ten thousand members who would seed the capital of one million to begin investments. Because of COVID-19, the goal was never met but the company was able to make two investments to date. Focusing on Webb Investment and CEEM while we tied up our next move as a family could have been a good move. Unfortunately, Kyle and my parents didn't see it that way.

My dad requested that for one year we would retain a handful of upper-level employees unless they found new jobs or chose to leave.

Most stayed. I felt this was okay as after a break I could reposition them within our new organization whatever it turned out to be. But with the uncertainty of our next move, this became a cost center with no revenue coming in to cover the salaries. We spent millions from the sales proceeds to do this, which meant depleting our resources. According to our estate plan, Kyle and I owned the lion's share of the company so it was our money going to pay the employees and Kyle did not think it a good business move so there was an urgency to move forward, and he was unhappy. A finance guy, he felt this was a ridiculous way to handle the issue and he could have been right because five million dollars later brought this disagreement to a head.

Still, I could not believe my ears when Kyle, out of the blue said, "Since there are no more McDonald's, and I am the CEO of Webb Investments and Webb Enterprises your services are no longer needed or valid and your skill set is not what is needed as we move forward." What that meant to him was my role would be to transition to being a part of the family office structure with voting rights, and not a part of the operations of what would come next, and what would come next would be under Webb Investments.

I was crushed. I wracked my brain to try to figure out where this vitriol could be coming from but couldn't. Did he really mean what he said? Did I misunderstand him? I started to rationalize. It might have come from the pressure I had put on him to live up to his role as the CFO of the McDonald's entities. Kyle, true to being the baby of the family who had experienced life quite differently from Karim and me, did not feel the same level of urgency to deliver on projects. When his projects were nearing nine months late, I had turned up the dial on the pressure for him to shape up. I was not sure if this was the root of his angst but what he said hurt so much. Unable to rebut, I walked away flinging angry words at Kyle. *Really, you think you can do better than me, go ahead and see if you can,* is what I thought but what I said was, "Okay Kyle, Good luck with that. I'm out! I'm over it." Those were my last words to my brother as I walked out of the family business. Karim was not in the business picture, but he too could not understand what could be going through Kyle's mind. Misunderstanding or not, a lot of the millions in his pockets were a direct result of my hard work!

As his words sunk in, I felt so unloved and underappreciated. I couldn't hold back the tears streaming down my face as they would for the next three months. The me, buried for too long under mountains of responsibilities and expectations could no longer ignore my pain. Deep down a voice rose louder and louder, clearer, and clearer: *You've fixed everything and everybody else, now it's time to fix you.*

Yes, I needed to find a way to love me. I wondered where God was in all of this. For months I sat on a sofa on my patio and cried. In those tears, the release of so much pressure, so many burdens, and so many disappointments flowed. For those months, every day my mind ran the same soliloquy:

I don't understand. Why would anyone treat me like I have no value? Dismiss me as though all my contributions were good enough then, but not good enough now? Does my history not prove my abilities? Why am I not enough for you as I am? Hadn't I filled coffers for life?

I was ashamed of my feelings. Guilt, shame, or was it anger, halted me in my tracks. I hoped it was anger because what did I have to be ashamed of? For thirty-five years I'd given my all to my family, never once asking for much. I'd worked damn hard. I'd put everyone before me. I'd acquiesced and sacrificed. Being so callously dismissed from my role as CEO, which I had categorically succeeded in, was a serious affront.

How dare he! If I had grown our family's business to unquestionable success, then, I could do the same for myself! Maybe it was indeed time to step aside. But what if I can't do it on my own? What if I fail?

Kiana! Stop thinking these thoughts! They are not helping at all!

But dammit, I did what was asked of me. I still do what is asked of me, so why does that not matter? Why, why, why? I'm tired of asking why. Tired of crying; tired of feeling sad and depressed fighting for something that doesn't want to be fought for. I am tired, too of striving to be what everyone wants me to be with no consideration as to who I truly am. I'm just plain tired. I'm on zero with nothing left to give. And after all the work I'd done where was this God I searched for?

God, why did he say those things? And why did he say them when I had not developed my spiritual armor fully and could only suppress how I felt? I'm back to the whys! I steered my mind in a different direction.

I thought this was your time to rest!

"But I cannot rest. There is beauty but no peace here." I begin an argument with God.

You said, be still and know.... What is there to know? That all my effort and life work had no value other than being a sibling? That's it? What does that even mean? Does it matter? Shoot, now I'm crying again. *I need help God. I'm tired. I just want to rest. Rest from the thoughts spiraling in my mind.*

Those days I just wanted peace and to feel loved for who I AM. Finding my path and discovering it for myself was the right thing to do. Being asked to step aside was the catalyst for my departure and it was a good decision. I now had time to figure out what I wanted to do with MY life, who I am in the bigger scheme of things, and what I wanted for my children without a single thought of what everyone else in the family needed. Maybe, as I had wished, this was the chance I needed to discover what I could do on my own. What I was made of outside of the family. To be honest I've wanted that more than anything but beyond being tired, I was a little scared of the unknown.

One day I was outside in my garden, tears unchecked, and I was tired. It was a beautiful day. I love the water fountain in my garden. The water gently ran its course in loops. I'd put it in some time ago because it made the space complete, yet I'd never had time to enjoy it. I love my home and I am so blessed. Above me, birds were singing their melodious songs. I looked up. With no appreciation for the danger, but clearly trust, I saw a flock of parrots landing on the electrical wires, their awful squawking quieting the soft, lyrical chirps of the other birds. For such beautiful creatures, their sound was awful. I laughed, appreciating the irony of it all. My feelings of anguish, the lush beauty of my surroundings and the beautiful beings of nature, some with melodious tunes and others with awful squawking, occupying the same space. My pain, hope, joy, and fear were occupying the same space, and it was okay. An epiphany.

One day, with nothing to do, nowhere to go, nothing to solve, no businesses to run, or the stress of listening to frantic people on the line calling me about emergencies that really weren't, I began to feel hopeful. "This is great," I exclaimed! "Why am I throwing a pity party when I got what I asked for?" I now have time to figure out what is next. I have three amazing young people to steward; I have time to write dance and play. Play? What's play? Do I even know how to play? Ok, maybe not play. But I could go on dates! Yes, I could date, plant a garden, fix up my house—the possibilities were endless. All the things I couldn't do before, I now have time to do.

For a while, however, I just sat there, uncertain. Kyle said he didn't want to be my business partner anymore and only wanted to have a relationship as a sibling. Well, maybe it was for the best. Maybe it was a good thing. After all, dad did the same for me. Stepped aside so I could take over, and that had worked out well. I had all the time in the world since I was told to step aside. And that's exactly what I did. Pity Kyle didn't appreciate my contribution.

I could enjoy my time—well, of course, I could do that. But it still hurt. Even in the beauty of my garden, it hurt. Why did this hurt so much? I am convincing myself there has to be a bigger purpose in all this because I don't think I can handle it anymore. This is too painful. My chest hurts. My heart, really. I can't take deep breaths; all I feel is pain coursing through my body. For a few more weeks I sat crying with nowhere to go and nothing to fix, no problems to solve. All the good things I had done are now gone and so was my self-esteem, again! Who am I without my title as CEO of Webb Enterprises?

My parents are calling telling me to fix it. I don't want it to be fixed. Karim, my other brother is trying to understand it. How can he understand it when I don't understand it myself? What's there to fix? What's to understand? Then I whispered, *please help me God*. I don't know what to do. I don't know who I am. I'm afraid, and I feel like I am losing my sense of self. I feel as if my whole world has no meaning. As if everything I lived for up until now has had no value. That my efforts, my sacrifices, and my endurance were all for naught. I'm experiencing grief like from a death and it comes with detachment from everything I thought I knew.

Elizabeth Kubler Ross says there are seven stages of grieving after death, I am only at stage one. How will I live through the next six? Being asked to step aside and land into a world of what is real has put me in a tailspin. I have walked away from what I perceived as my life and from the only me I've ever known, and I am lost.

After repeated calls from my dad telling me this is not time to have a conflict with Kyle, once again I give in. I called Kyle and told him we needed to have a conversation.

The day had not started out like any other, because I had been relieved of my job I was not bustling to get breakfast ready or to get my kids to school. I didn't have to head to the office to do my job as CEO of Webb Family Enterprises. Kyle said he could talk in thirty minutes on his way home. I knew the conversation could be heated so I decided to drive to the park about two miles from my home to take the call. I walked to a nearby tree and sat on the grass to ground myself. I went over and over in my head what I would say and having the benefit of some spiritual maturity I prayed I would yield to compassion and listen without judgment to what my brother had to say. The phone call from Kyle changed everything. I heard but couldn't process what he was saying. Cell phone to my ear, I was frozen in shock when Kyle uttered the words.

I have been everything else to Kyle, his mother, friend, sister, and business partner. Being reduced to just a sister was insulting. I had no idea what that meant anyway as I had always related to him as my child. The air around me shifted to stillness. My eyes blurred and my head spun. Everything I had prayed for flew out the window. As the second person in my life, I'd screamed at, beside my husband Paul, I screamed at Kyle until I was prostrate. Enraged, I reminded him of why his behavior had been unacceptable in his job. I reminded him this was not personal but business. I reminded him of all the things I had created that he had benefited from, and I reminded him I was waiting to hear an explanation for his vile statements. But all I heard was a click as the line went dead. Had my brother really just hung up? With the silent phone still pressed to my ear, I broke into a million little pieces. I am not sure how I made it home but when I got to my bedroom I didn't trust my legs to hold me up, so I sank to the bare wooden floor. I had known for a long time the many factors that led to where we were now. I truly did, but to think I'd poured my heart and soul into Kyle since the day he was born when I was merely seven and a half years old, only made me sadder. I was the one to change his diapers. I was the one to wrestle him into his highchair and get him his food. I was the one who taught him how to tie his shoelaces and I was the one to take care of him when my mom couldn't, and my dad was working. And I hadn't regretted it at all. I loved it. Loved him. And now he didn't want anything to do with me.

My mind raced through the months and years that had brought us here. What could I have done differently? Why was this happening now? The child to whom I had devoted my life had said, "Kiana, I do not want to be in business with you, I do not want to be your friend, I only want to relate to you as a sister and that's it."

I was a solid businesswoman. That I knew, with absolute certainty. It truly hurt my heart when my brother undermined my contribution to the family that had finally and resolutely returned the kind of wealth only a few had the privilege of expecting. The truth was, and is, I love my family. As dysfunctional and suppressed as we might be, they are my family and without a shadow of a doubt, I love them dearly. But this was a hard pill to swallow. I went back into my cocoon and cut off all communication with my family while I processed my own next steps. Never once did I see that Kyle's outburst would lead to the next step of my spiritual growth, landing me in front of the God I sought.

As I sat with myself, I was aware I had to lay bare my hidden soul for the journey ahead I had to face. It was on this very day my body asked my heart how do I heal the hurt? How do I repair the shattered little girl inside the cocoon? How do I find the me I wanted to be? I had to heal by myself in my way, and without truly realizing it, I silently thanked my brother because he was the catalyst, and it was time—time to find the real me. Without my job, my family, my perception of self; who was I? And where do I start to find out? It was not until writing this book that I got full clarity about my interaction with my brother.

In my family, we learned to solve problems through what I call logic-ing. Feelings and emotions were not a part of our toolbox. That my brother could have been asking for something other than what I heard was something I could not see. Had I had spiritual vision I would have seen and heard things not being said. What I see now is the truth. Kyle rejected me because he needed to find his footing. I now see how I wielded my *cross to bear* story as my control over my family. I see too how my mother's refusal to face her truth because as she said, she "might not like what she saw" kept her silent, and I see my older brother Karim's rejection of the duplicity we practiced. I see my father's need to control all around him in our family which blocked two-way communication as there was no room for emotional exchanges, objections, or otherwise. I could now sit with these revelations. To release the deep and true love we had for each other we needed to unearth our truths. To find a solution to my emotional stagnation, I needed to find unconditional love, a love that just is for my family. Without judgment or blame, my family, who'd given their all in the way they knew how, did the best they could. After all, I had chosen them for a reason, and true to the promise, through them, I found the courage to step into my light. Had it not been for my brother's need for his freedom, I could have wavered longer. I was forced to face the ordeal his anger created, and it was unpleasant. Of course, when it happened, I had no idea why it did, and I was super angry. My ego had been deeply wounded and in defense, I was forced to make a choice. Being ill-informed of the true source of the problem, coupled with our sense of importance, led to decisions that had we been more spiritually mature, could have been avoided. Only after I started group therapy did I find the courage to cross the bridge of our shared humanity. It might have shown up as anger and frustration, but his detonation kicked me out of my discomfort zone. I'd had many glimpses into the possibility of returning to self, but none had offered this quite seemingly simple solution to the Why of my life. I realized that I could get out of my cocoon, pack up all my pain, disappointment, fear, and anger and leave them behind in the storm; that I could choose to be a light in the world, and that I would become free as me. Because I AM.

Trauma Responses

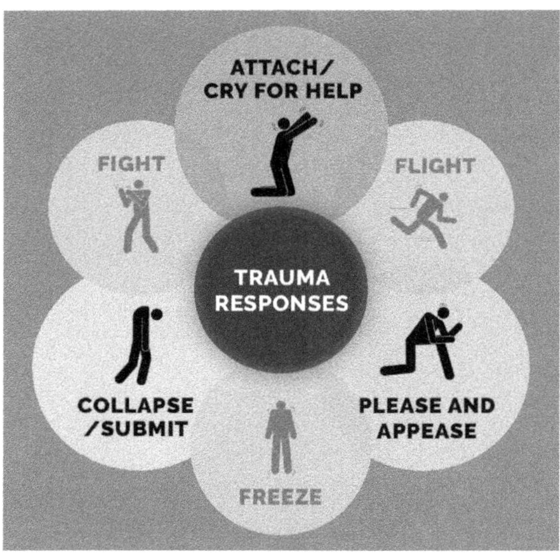

Reprinted with the permission of original creator NICABM

Trauma can show up in myriad ways.
The above diagram shows the obvious and less obvious
ways in which we deal with trauma.
Try to identify your trauma response.

PART II

THE KEYS FAITH, HOPE AND LOVE IN ACTION

CHAPTER EIGHT
THE JOURNEY

☥

I GOT THE TIME OFF I NEEDED because I took it and at the time could have cared less what my family thought. By now, I know the pain I was feeling was transmuted fear. Fear of walking alone; of standing on the other side of something unknown. It is a journey I had to take because deep down I already knew that if I didn't cross over to the other side of me, I would die to the hope, faith, and love of my yet unrealized potential. I had long been certain I couldn't have stayed in the place of the known because it always felt like a prison. My protective shell of unworthiness, guilt, and shame had been straining. It was ready to explode unless my imagination and deep-down strength could find a way to carry me across, or a cosmic kick gave me a jumpstart. So why was I grieving when I've always wanted to find me? Because I was afraid of letting go of the vice grip I had on who I thought I was; afraid to be all I was meant to be. Afraid of a love that had no expectations, conditions, or rules. Afraid of loving the powerful me who could heal, sing, dance, and celebrate the fullness of life. Now I'd come face-to-face with the fact that I was afraid to be me and that I was trapped in a prison of my own making, still too afraid to break free.

Before Kyle's cosmic kick woke me up, I was truly stuck in the middle of what was and what could be. I needed to surrender to a love beyond my understanding. To receive peace that surpassed all my pain. To find grace in my life. It was time to pull the curtain wide open and begin the transformative process of finding me. A new world would open up to me in my next group therapy.

I found it hard to believe I was the architect of my suffering. This was too philosophical an idea for me to grasp. *Landmark Forum* illuminated that since I was a little girl, like Nana, I had always been searching for a love found outside of me. Even with my failed relationships, I kept waiting and waiting for my prince to save me, much like I kept searching for my light to heal me.

To find the me I was looking for I had to return to my innocence at birth which had been conditioned out of me through the years. I was in search of the five-year-old me who used to talk so much people would leave the room to get a break from my incessant talking. Where had she gone? As I had grown quieter and quieter from learning to suppress my feelings and not show my true emotions, I'd learned to "suck it up." The moment I'd felt a need to cry I'd shut down, knowing my dad would say, "Don't cry or else I'll give you something to really cry about." Even on the rare occasions when I wanted to share all of what was storming inside my body, there was nowhere to go. If what I had to say sounded like a complaint, my mom would say, "If you don't have anything nice to say don't say anything at all."

Facing me meant recognizing that at a young age, I had already figured out how to channel my unvoiced, pent-up frustration. Emotionally shut down and burdened, I didn't have the emotional or psychological language to recognize a love that didn't require me to give. The cues of the love I understood were buried under mountains of responsibilities and inappropriate experiences. Giving away all of me to others was my desire to be loved. Never once had I recognized that my physicality, me, could attract love without me giving something in return.

I remember once I was at the movies with my cousin. I was only twelve but as usual, no one could tell. I was wearing Levis and a T-shirt and since we'd walked about two miles from my home to get to the movie theater, I was sweaty. My long, straight hair, either pressed or permed, was in a ponytail as it was the easiest style for me to manage. I wasn't trying to look special. A size twelve, 5' 10" with big curvaceous hips and a small waist, I had to cinch my belt, so my super baggy pants hugged my hips and didn't fall down. I was unaware of my beauty. I would never have fathomed anyone would be attracted to me, especially since I was always dressed in men's pants and size twelve men's tennis shoes. I did have one blessing, my complexion remained clear into my thirties, but it didn't seem to help my love life. If you look at pictures from my teen-age years and look at me now, you wouldn't see much of a difference. A little bit more maturity, yeah, but I've always had a youthful face and my responsibilities made me carry myself older than I was and there was always wisdom written on my face.

Because of being molested in my early childhood, I had never allowed myself to be touched. I always kept my emotional and physical guard on high alert, so in puberty, a time of learning the nuances of liking a boy and a boy liking me back never happened. I was clueless about this guy's advances. Apparently, the guy who seemed to like me was not bothered by my attire or height and was following me around. When he wouldn't stop trailing us my cousin finally turned around and screamed at him, "She's only twelve." The thing is, I hadn't even noticed him. Since my love radar had never sprouted, I was clueless to understand innocent flirtation. Fully developed by age twelve as a woman, the guy would never have imagined me a typical middle school student, except maybe for my buck teeth! Once my teeth were straightened, people only saw me as a grown-up. It didn't help that I also carried myself with a dignity instilled by my parents and was able to communicate effectively with anyone. The poor guy thought, like everyone else, I was an adult.

Not much changed for me as an adult. A broken engagement and failed marriage made the prospect of finding the nurturing love I imagined seem impossible. Because very few people were allowed in my inner circle, dinner party "set up" meetings were not the norm. Even today, as much as I wish to be coupled, my protective radar still finds its way out in my relationships.

At thirty-six years old, I realized I truly didn't understand love. My abuse had left me unable to form intimate relationships, so I began mulling over all the lessons I'd taken away from the *Landmark Forum*. What if I could set my intention and shift my perspective from a place of pain and depression to joy and fulfillment? If I wanted to find a fulfilling and loving relationship, I needed to move the needle on my self-discovery forward.

I had first seen a therapist when I was twenty-four, but I had been to the school psychologist in high school when my mother was relentless in trying to make me perfect. Back then I was not ready to deal with the reality of my repression, so I ended it after one session. Had I been able to look at my reality, I would have seen my mother's need to feel useful in our family. My perfection was it. The story she had told herself is, that I was additive to my father and the mother of Kyle, so her role was to make me perfect. This made me a nervous wreck and I retreated even more.

There was no way now for me to reclaim myself without going through the storm. Over the years, I had ignored the little hurts that turned into big hurts and then into the boulders that steamrolled my life, setting up the perfect conditions for a storm-turned-hurricane to come rolling in. In the storm, I was hauling unnecessary baggage filled with fear, anger, hatred, frustration, disappointment, and bitterness. Learning that even in the midst of the hurricane, to be calm meant staying at the center of the storm (the eye of the storm) through destruction that swirled and decimated all in its path. I had to stay there to find a state of detachment. I had to leave the baggage along the way to be consumed by the raging storm. The truth, however, was that the destruction was my creation to rid myself of traumas and burdens. However, from a state of detachment at the center of the storm, I found I could look at destruction and still find comfort, peace, and contentment no matter the category of the hurricane. From the storm's eye, I was a mindful observer at a gateway into my soul and could influence what would affect my life. Because of the impermanence of things in almost every aspect of life, including birth and death, living with detachment, mindfulness, and self-discipline are prerequisites for a fulfilling life. Eventually, the storm subsides.

Today, I am living proof debilitating emotional pain can be a catalyst for self-discovery. I caution, however, that finding oneself does not mean a life without pain or disappointments. But doing the work, and investing the time needed to return to self-love, can lead to skills and tools for facing fear head-on. When the light of awareness illuminates the dark corners of denial, the courage to stand firm in the face of fear can begin the journey of looking inward. Lucky for me no matter how hard I tried to ignore the obvious, my soul calling was like a persistent nag that never gave up.

Over the years little clues would pop up reminding me I was an outlier, not by choice, but by experience and I should embrace myself as I AM. No matter how broken, and despondent I felt, I was ready to build a life of harmony and reclaim my authentic self. Through being able to understand my unique design, examine my values, assess my abilities, listen to my gut, and manage disturbing memories, I'd come a long way and was certain the love I desired would come. Loving and accepting oneself is a precondition for loving others unconditionally.

I will not lie. It was hard work. It was a monumental climb to combat my fears and I was petrified of opening the door of enlightenment. What would happen if I opened up my emotions? Would it be like opening a Pandora's box? Would I go insane? I was deathly afraid of going crazy; of being institutionalized from a nervous breakdown. I was terrified my family, especially my parents, would think I was blaming them for my life of turmoil. Hurting them or being a disappointment to them was nothing I wanted to experience. It was better to disappoint myself. I vacillated between my options. I kept thinking a futile journey might have broken me wide open and I would be unable to put myself back together again.

Facing the cause of my disquietude was daunting and the fear of looking at myself paralyzing. Since I'd yearly added new layers of self-protection, how far would I have to dig to hit my truth? The little light I'd been born with had long been snuffed out and wading through layers and layers of doubt, fear, anger, guilt, shame, and lack of self-worth would surely test my mettle. But staying where I was would surely kill me in the worst way. I would continue to be a walking dead. I did nothing for a while. I stayed stuck.

But time had run out for me. I was at the end of my runway. There could be no more hiding from myself. I was well aware I was way different on the inside than I was perceived, and my inner and outer selves did not match. For me to survive, I had to take the plunge. The years of suppressing everything about me had come to a screeching halt. The truth is, I didn't know where to begin. Had it not been for my brother's explosion, and his invitation, I could still have been in my cocoon. Looking back, I'm grateful for every moment, every experience, and every interaction I had because they all led me to this moment in life, allowing me to share with you.

It's now the spring of 2021, and things have opened up, so travel is once again possible. I had been wanting to experience an ayahuasca ceremony since my first time in plant medicine therapy. Ayahuasca is not something to do unless the spirit calls you. I knew I was called when Ayahuasca appeared to me in a vision with her black panther during a plant medicine ceremony. I began asking around about Ayahuasca. Somebody directed me to Peru and a few different places, but I wasn't exactly feeling them. A year later, I was talking to a mutual friend, Atila, who happened to mention that his wife did yoga retreats in Costa Rica, and though they had never done plant medicine, they knew of a place there where I could go.

I took the next step and traveled in the Spring of 2021 to Costa Rica to a treatment center called Rythmia Life Advancement Center in the northern part of Costa Rica, Guanacaste. My intention when I got there was to just love bigger than all my fears. From the moment I was picked up at the airport, handed a snack and water, and greeted by a canopy of trees on the drive to the sprawling tropical compound, I knew I was in for something special. At Rythmia, mind, body, and spirit are cared for in an all-inclusive, luxurious environment (it was needed—believe me), with farm-to-table organic meals, healing massages, dance, yoga, breath work, and so much more under the care of medically licensed physicians and plant medicine specialists focused on awaking the dormant spirit. This included Ayahuasca ceremonies. I had been part of the plant-based community long enough to have experienced an ayahuasca blend, but I was most curious about Ayahuasca. Ayahuasca is not a medicine but a spiritual practice one has to be called to. I spent my first time at Rythmia detoxing from the outside world. Through meditation, breath work, deep cleansing, magnificent organic food, and nature, I aimed to get in touch with myself and my feelings, shut down for way too long.

My awakening in Costa Rica with Ayahuasca was a four-day magical and exhausting experience. The first day was lovely. I was floating among these beautiful pastel pinatas. It felt like I was in the middle of the ocean amongst all the different flora and fauna but with no water! My body had a slight buzz, and I was just floating. On the second day, the vision went from pastels, lovely and gentle to a little bit of a stinging buzz. By the end of the second day, I was being asked to let go. As much as I was trying, I just couldn't do it. At the end of the ceremony, I was exhausted. I'm not sure of the concoctions I was given each day, but on the third day, the intensity of the feeling was intense. I could hear my guide asking me once again to release what I needed to release. Considering the intention, I'd gone with, to love bigger than my fear, so far my fear was winning.

For every ceremony we entered, there were three intentions they'd take you through, the first asked the medicine to show who you are at all costs and how the world sees you, based on what you've been projecting. The second was to heal the heart and unlock the compartments unavailable because of fear. At the center of discontent, they contended, is the inability to feel what's in one's heart. How to understand what it means for my heart to be open is my work. The funny thing is, I always heard a lot about an open heart in church, but it's one thing to do it logically and quite another to do it spiritually. I'd had a glimpse into an open heart with both Kyle and Samia. The third was to connect me to my soul. I trusted the process and I tried so hard, then just like that, this beautiful pulsing glow came over me; it emanated from within me and it felt like I was exuding or secreting some sort of chemical that made me feel good, and happy to be alive. My heart opened and even now as I'm writing about this, I just want to curl up in its warmth and stay here. It just felt so good to feel how good my heart felt. In this state, I didn't want to hurt or harm people or myself because my heart was open and receiving and I knew whatever I give I will receive. This is the benefit of just living in love, which was my intention. Once the medicine was over, I unfortunately found myself going back to my old habits of living in my comfort zone of fear and pain. Did I do all this for naught? Not quite.

The fourth day is the end of the ceremony. I am going into a healing circle. I had been holding on so tight to the past for the first three days, and by this time I was so exhausted. I didn't know what to do. On Ayahuasca, the body eliminates toxicity, and I was becoming nauseous and vomiting a lot. My gastrointestinal system was in overdrive and as I ran to the bathroom, I prayed no one was ahead of me. I found it incredulous that from three ounces of medicine taken, the body could eliminate three times so much waste from every orifice. I knew it was a part of what the medicine was doing—purging me of all of the things blocking my spiritual progress, relieving me from the dis-ease that can often turn disease, but it was intense. The shaking, the sweating, the laughing, the crying, and the screaming, were all part of the elimination of stored energy in my body that no longer served me.

I am given a number for the healing circles to join. Aligned in a circle on the floor are pillows. There are thirty to forty people in the space. The head shaman and his team lead a ritual of healing which includes the use of tonics, sprays, smoke, feathers, and leaves along with chants and taps to the body with the feathers and leaves as they increase the energy of the room through vibrational sound and movement.

As I'm sitting in this healing circle I just know I'm going to be sick. I was anxious to leave and squirming when all of a sudden, I expelled this clear, foul-smelling liquid that just kept flooding my whole system. When it was finally over I felt such relief, but I was soaking wet, basically from my belly button down to my toes, and the smell was atrocious. More than appalled, I felt an overwhelming feeling of shame. I wanted to get up, but I couldn't. I'm somehow rooted. My spiritual healer comes and starts doing ritual healing on me. I'm embarrassed, no, mortified because of the smell from my body. I am soaking wet and to make matters worse it's no longer the middle of the night! With the dawn breaking, I'm supposed to get up from my pillow in front of the circle and walk back to my mattress, letting everyone know I lost control of myself. The crushing shame that left my body was the toxicity I was holding onto but had no idea was there. Suddenly, as I was taking my walk of shame, a part of me wanted to celebrate! I felt proud to have expelled such shame. I just wanted to parade around the room and say look at me! I just shed all of this shame that feels like shit, smells like shit, and probably is shit! Then just as quickly I went back into my head, tucked my body in protective mode, in complete embarrassment and back into shame.

I finally got up and one of the helpers escorted me to my room. I took a much-needed shower. As I came out of the stall, my eyes fall upon the beautiful saying on the wall. There is a wall plaque with sayings in every room. I believe when you get there, though not by design, one is put in the room with a message exactly right for you. My message was, "The only way out is through."

I had been through it; of that I was sure. I felt like a wrung-out doll. First of all, at this point, I hadn't slept for twenty-two hours. I lie down, the effects of the plant medicine still lingering and I'm in a state of emotional upheaval. It's now late morning, breakfast has passed, and

I didn't eat but I did go to the first session which was the integration class. I'm wrapped in a blanket and I'm miserable and crying. There are few people at this session and it's a relief. Because we've been up all night, and it is exhausting, and because we've just finished four days of ceremony people took time to be with themselves. During class, the facilitator asked me, "Are you okay?"

"No, I'm not."

And so, when the class was over, she came and sat with me. I told her what had happened and I was sobbing.

"Humm, well, let's reframe this."

I looked at her and I said, "I can't."

And she goes, "Well, yes, you can."

"I can't reframe this one," I said, "because I have to walk through it. Because the only way I'm going to heal from this is if I truly allow myself to feel it—to go through it." And right there, for the first time in my life, I understood what it meant to sit still. To sit in it, to sit in the shame, to sit in the years of disquietude, to review it, to stare at it, and to fully accept it. The way back through meant fully accepting all that has happened to me; all the stories I created; all the limiting beliefs I held onto because of those stories; all the pain and shame—being in acceptance of it all. Once I did that and got past the fear of really looking at myself, I went back to my room. I cried and cried and cried until there were no more tears. I put a towel down so scared of having any bodily mishaps and I was finally able to rest.

For the next day and a half, I went to all the events. Every single class worked to reduce the energy of shame inhabiting my body and as it left, my soul felt lighter. But it wasn't just my soul because when I got back on the scale, I was ten pounds lighter than when I had arrived. And there it was. I had lost ten pounds of dis-ease stored in my body. From the time I was a child until that moment, I had been disconnected from my soul. I was cut off from love's frequency and here I was, seven days after I arrived at Rythmia feeling so much freedom and so much love and knew my healing had reached another level.

Healing is not a logical experience, it is the combination of a physical, spiritual, and mental awakening reconnecting our disconnected souls. At the end of my first stay, I'd unlocked a new level of understanding of all the things I had accepted and owned that were holding me back from the love and light within me. I wasn't dead. I just hadn't allowed my emotions free reign. I had logic-ed my life to death.

As the CEO of Webb Enterprises for over fifteen years, given to rational thinking, if you had told me this was a journey I would have embarked on even ten years before, I would have said "aw, hell no!" And I'd bet against you to lose. Then it dawned on me that we think nothing of taking medicines to heal our physical ailments, so why not medicine to heal our emotional ailments? This was another launching point in my knowing and awareness. My journey was to become free of all the negative energies that attached themselves to my body, allowing me to be all I was born to be. I had no further need to defend my actions. They were mine, pure and simple, and I was entering a new phase of freedom.

At the end of my journey, I would come to understand everything that happened to me was by design. It was meant to happen for the lessons I needed to learn in this lifetime. And everything that happened is the reason why I am who I am today, and I wouldn't change any of it. When I confronted my fears and reimagined my perspective, the magic of my life began to unfold.

Not everyone wants to rise to the occasion of doing the work, but I am here to nudge you because in doing the work you will find your true self and have the ability to unlock your unique, divine gifts to further enhance the joy in being who you are meant to be. The inner peace that comes from self-knowledge is priceless. Rather than striving to attain tangible things as defined by our society (such as money, homes, cars, and clothes), which are external, inner peace leads to personal freedom. When we understand who we are, we are truly effecting change in the world, creating a global reset that shifts our collective consciousness to a higher level. Being one's true self means being certain of who you are regardless of your or others' expectations and influence over you—regardless of your job description.

Getting to know oneself is a lifelong journey. There is no one-size-fits-all way to get there because it is a personal walk. I had embarked on a journey and from many healing groups I learned to trust the process as I began to discover the awakened Kiana. Feeling secure and convinced about my discoveries, I most importantly got my answer to who God is. I used to think God was outside in a destination I needed to go to, but what I am absolutely certain of now is we all come from God, we all return to God, and at no time do we live separated from God because God is me and who I am is God. Though we've never been separated, we have been disconnected.

Going through my healing journey was one of the hardest things I've ever done for myself, but for the first time in my life I was beginning to feel whole. My understanding of my pain dramatically shifted the trajectory of my life and the lives of those in my sphere when I came to accept I was not a victim but a soul on its way journeying back to self. As horrific as it might seem, being abused at such an early age, having to be responsible, being an anomaly, or having limiting beliefs; these were the paths I needed to be on to find my way back to Source. If you were to ask me now to define the larger context of my personal story, I would say, Love Is All There Is. We are meant to forget so that we can remember. We are meant to disconnect so that when we reconnect to an expanded version of ourselves which increases our capacity to love and the capacity to all love. The even larger context of my personal story was to rediscover the love I AM always.

From daily aspirational bombardments, one of the falsehoods people have been living under in modern times is that life should always be happy and rewarding. Happiness, like any other emotion, however, is never a permanent state. Emotions ebb and flow, giving us clues as to who we are and the lessons we need to pay attention to, to remember ourselves. The remembrance of who we are and being in full acceptance of that with love, I believe unlocks the kind of peace and joy that defies logic.

On my remembrance journey I learned two of the most valuable lessons: first, everything happens for a reason and though this may be hard to believe, I wouldn't change any of it. For as my soul is reemerging back to itself, I am finding a joy I never thought possible; second, self-love, and this is a biggie. Learning self-love gives the ability to accept people for who they are because everyone is worthy and beautiful and deserving of grace. Acceptance is in itself magical. Acceptance of people means you've accepted yourself and you're connected at a deep emotional level to Source. In doing so you'll be unable to intentionally harm anyone, including yourself.

From the beginning of my journey in 2005 when I consciously chose to change until now, at times it has seemed like a long walk to my joy and peace. But I know real joy is possible because I experience it daily. Joy, as opposed to fleeting happiness, is a deep feeling that comes from within, and it is not dependent on external circumstances. Even so, a real sense of joy is not something that can always be controlled but there are things that can be done to increase our chances of experiencing it. By focusing on things important to us, by building strong relationships, and by cultivating a positive outlook on life, we can create a foundation for real joy.

I can only speak of the shift I experienced going on my journey into self with the idea of a return to love as a core tenet. It proved to be a shift in my perspective. By changing the way, I thought and felt about things opened a path for me to walk. What was magical was the liberating feeling that came from listening only to my inner voice. I was therefore able to claim and accept things that were for me and reject the things that were not.

Returning from my second and last trip to Rythmia where I had done massive trauma work in 2022, and in 2023 shredded shame, was cathartic. I had changed a lot and had reached a level of spiritual maturity. To my surprise, but not really, when I came home wanting to shine my newly found light into the dark corners of my existence, I was met with resistance. Conflict within myself and my family made me simply stop talking. I silently quit carrying the victim's story, stopped asking, blaming, or waiting for approval, and began observing and listening more to all that was going on around me. Instead of explaining and complaining I got acquainted with life on my terms. I have never enjoyed unnecessary drama and therefore was no longer a co-conspirator to our family's dysfunction.

The benefits of my journey were so worth it, they far outweighed the fears. I pushed forward silently. The challenge with continuing this work, especially since my core wounding was family, was especially hard. However, I didn't give up and continued to move in the direction of my freedom even though I didn't always feel supported in my journey. Even writing this book was a challenge because there are things my family will not appreciate, but I know these are my truths and as a spiritual being in progress, truth is all I can offer.

My family was upset that I would take the time to focus on my spiritual well-being when we were running a business, selling one, buying one, and raising my children; yet I never bowed to the pushback. I was doing this for me because I wanted to have a healthier relationship with my family and that had to be based on my truths. I wanted to be more engaged with my mother. I wanted to take time out with my friends, and I wanted time to play. This was my expression of self-love, and I was determined to create it. In reconnecting to Source, the gifts I received allowed me to have a new language, a new vision, and a new understanding and opened the door for others to begin their reconnecting journey, including members of my family.

The things I learned from my journey were powerful.

1. Emotions are a gateway to let you know if you are connected or disconnected from yourself or others.
2. Everywhere I felt disconnected was a place where there was work to be done.

3. In loving bigger than my fear, the only thing I needed to change was believing in and claiming myself and that all things were possible.

4. The Power of Belief is the power of I AM. Every human being is a creator.

5. We only see partial truths.

6. How to transmute the stories I held on to as pain into pleasure.

7. I had to let go of control to get everything I ever wanted.

8. The purpose of life is to be itself.

9. That everything, even though it might not feel good, is good for you.

10. God talks to us all the time.

11. Nature is powerful for our healing.

12. We all know our truth.

Me at 1 Year old.

Me at 4 Years old.

Me at 2 Years old.

Me in the 5th Grade.

Me, 7 ½ Years Old, and Kyle 2 months old.

Me at 9, Kyle at 2 ½ Years Old.   Me 20, Kyle 14.

Me High School Freshman
Year, 1992.

Me Senior Year, 1996.

Me and Craig at my Graduation.

My Graduation: Mama Mat, Craig, Me, Rene(Mom) Aunty Leonear.

Me, 2018.   Me, 2022.

Mom, Geraldine Rene Webb.

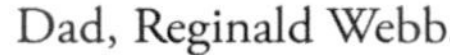

Dad, Reginald Webb.

Brother, Kyle Webb.

Brother, Karim Webb.

Me, Dad, Kyle.

Me, VP Kamala Harris, and Dad.

Me receiving the WFE honor at The University of La Verne Gala.

Me, communing with nature.

Kyle and Me being interviewd for a podcast at the
Drucker Graduate School of Business by host, Kathleen Farriss.

Meeting with the team at the Webb office.

Left to right: Dad, Mom, me, my husband Paul, Garnet Paul's Mom, Adolf "Butch" Severloh, Paul's dad, Sharon Brown, Butch's life partner.

Me, Paul, and their son Jason, 4 months old.

Jason, Sanai, me, Samia During COVID went to Costa Rica for remote work and school; 2021

Sanai and me at Queen concert.

Samia and me making brownies.

Parents' 50th wedding anniversary, Mom, and me.

Attending a wedding: Mom, me holding Kemmet Kyle, and Amy's son, Samia, Amy, Sanai, and Kyle.

Kyle, Mom, Dad, me, Karim, December 2022.

Me and Amy, not my birthday. It's everyone's birthday party.

In my backyard with Spike, my dog.

Amy, my constant companion and emotional support.

Me, meditating on my patio
where I cry a lot.

Soul sister, Mercedes Marroquin,
and me in Costa Rica.

Me being with nature.

Me, relaxing in my living room.

Me owning my style.

Me: Embracing my power.

Dear Reader,

Part three of this book shares with you some of the tools and practices that were helpful to me on my journey. As you go deeper into part three, there may be ideas and concepts with which you may not be familiar. One such is, when we come into this world as human beings our soul enters into a divine contract with the universal source, The I AM. It's a choice we've made in a previous existence now long forgotten but still needs completion. Of course, this is one theory about existence but whatever your belief system, you are here.

I was born fully realized, loving myself, and completely free to be me. As with all of us, life experiences led me to forget who I am. This change shouldn't be so hard to imagine as it can be observed in the transformation of humans from birth to early childhood and beyond. As newborns, who are completely free to be themselves, dependency on caregivers puts them at the mercy of the love, commitment, and trust of those entrusted to feed, cuddle, clothe, and teach them. The soundness of care determines the child's love and appreciation of self. If love is not fully realized in the caregiver, the child will begin to live into the demands and expectations of those in charge of their well-being. Constant inner commentary on how they measure up, outer social conditioning, and life expectancies of others, change them and the freedom they once had will be forgotten. In other words, what it means to be their true selves becomes lost in growing up.

I, like others, created a story that kept me safe. I spun a cocoon of forgetfulness, or so I thought to protect my inner being. Now I have come to understand that those defensive behaviors, those I am aware of and those I am not, have kept me disconnected from what I've wanted most—being and experiencing love; being free again. They were also gifts that kept me protected as I was learning and developing. Because of those protections and the resulting disconnection from loving, I gained significant wisdom and knowledge; they were gifts that shaped me and brought resiliency, and the strength that helped me heal. In doing spiritual work, I noticed the freer I became the more I connected to love and to the realization that everything is in divine order. Though it may not seem like it, everything that happens, the parts you like, and those you don't, are in perfect order and designed to expand the evolutionary consciousness of love. As a mother I used to think I couldn't love any child more than my first one. When my second and third children were born, my capacity to love expanded, and the thought that it could never be, was just a story I made up. Expansive love is exactly how I experience the love I now have for myself, for others, and for all things. In all ways, and in all experiences, every place that I didn't think I could love more, or deeper, was always available.

In the search for the authentic soul, research suggests that the most asked question is, Why am I here? I used to ask myself the very question along with; Why has this happened to me; What is the meaning of it all; and What's the purpose and lesson of my existence? I came to accept the pain bodies I carried around from my perception that I was not enough; that I had to be responsible for my family; that I was a bother if I asked for help; and when things didn't go right, that it was my fault, just to name a few, were albatrosses. These perceptions became my reality and I often felt stuck and out of place.

Neither moving forward nor backward I was on pause. No! I was stuck. Until I understood the spiritual truths that kept showing up in my life, I was unable to recognize the I AM keys that unlocked the door to my realized soul. My awakening came with accepting that I had always been walking in my purpose and the reason for being here was simply to be me. Every life experience I had needed to happen to fulfill my soul contract and lead me to my Glorious Arising. Until I began my healing I could not comprehend that what I went through, everything that happened, was to raise my vibration and understanding of the differences in the human world we live in, and the spiritual world we come from. Did I lose you here? Maybe. But don't worry. Journey along with me in Faith, Hope, and Love, suspend disbelief, give up the need to control outcomes, and simply allow yourself to be.

Someone said to me once that they just wanted to be loved bigger than their fears. My initial response was, how could one love you bigger than your fear? Isn't that your job to love yourself bigger than your fears? How could anyone else love you bigger than that? The chance of that happening is only possible if we are able to love ourselves greater than all our fears. That statement however stirred something in me. I began to ask myself the question, "Do I love bigger than my fears?" The answer was a resounding no and that was very hard to face. But even harder to face was the fact that, in so many ways, I didn't love myself at all.

What I have come to learn is that my capacity to love bigger than my fears begins with me. I am *the* somebody who needs to find unconditional love—a love that has no conditions, expectations, or judgments. What I think I should be, who I think I am, and who I think others are, fall within this kind of love that grants a peace that surpasses all understanding. Because unconditional love is always grounded in the ever-present divine love, it is always present when we reconnect to it on the journey of returning to self—a return to love, the place where we love bigger than all our fears.

With Faith, Hope, Love, and Glorious Arisings,
Kiana Webb

PART III

OPEN

CHAPTER NINE
RUMBLE

☥

IN A WORLD THAT REWARDS uniformity, straying off the beaten path is often frowned upon. But to live in one's true essence and reconnect to the Divine Matrix, to endeavor to change both personal and global realities, a spiritual awakening is likely to occur. In this section of the book, I will share some of the conventional wisdom prevailing around a spiritual awakening as well as the lessons that personally resonated with me as I journeyed toward my soul's remembrance. I hope through these spiritual lessons you will come to realize the Universe is always guiding you to choose the path to remembrance, and when we don't, dis-ease and disease come into our lives.

There is no single way to a spiritual awakening, but there will however be commonalities, and those are what I will share—a few of the philosophies and teachings I follow which are rooted in the concepts of Faith, Hope, and Love, my pathways to my Glorious Arising.

Within the quest for spiritual fulfillment, is a new spiritual language you will learn. To get to the clarity that you are, and always have been whole, you'll need to trust the spiritual path you are on and embrace the revelations on your journey. This will undoubtedly test your understanding of reality as this new language reinforces that the source of empowerment lies within, and is in fact, your very essence; the conscious soul. Conscious living sheds the weight and shackles of an ego-bound life and brings you face-to-face with who you truly are in the eyes of God.

If seeking a life of fulfillment with joy is your aim, the why of the Why and your desire to have your longing answered are in the discovery of your ultimate self. To live in a state of joyful bliss is the result of seeing yourself in the full experience and expression of your own life. For me, this is a place where I can fully express the reason for my existence. I AM that I AM. Recognition of the I AM means I have fully claimed, and am in communication with self, others, and with Source, which is and creates the oneness of the I AM. Arriving at a Glorious Arising you experience a sense of awe, wonder, and curiosity at discovering your true essence and the miracle of who you are.

This is the time when your ego, fighting and kicking pushes hard for your limiting beliefs to sabotage the fullness of the creation you are building. My pastor used to say the sign is not the thing, the sign is the thing that points to the thing. Sabotage will ultimately lose because whatever it is you're setting out to create, you have invoked certainty and are now living from a place of all-knowing that does not require placing any tactical or tangible outcome into it. You are placing the experience of what you're setting out to create above the outcome; therefore, when the "what's the reason for" question is asked by others, there will be little need for an answer. A question about "reason for" is like asking the waves shaping the rocks and nourishing the life it holds above and within it, where it is going. Doesn't that depend on the conditions of the stream that silently provides its power? The question then of what is shaping us becomes extraneous. People will stop asking irrelevant questions as you begin to silently manifest the power of who you are.

As you journey down your path you'll find the track you're on has already been in your heart. The feelings, expressions of love, how you want to feel, and how you want to experience life the way you want for yourself, are on that track. There's a verse in the Bible that says, "Put God above all things." When the time comes and you meet your God-self, you'll have realized that you have put your I AM-self above all things and you are in direct communication with Source. Being in the spirit of who you are creates a protection against the ego which seeks to keep us rooted in the behaviors and thoughts of our ego-selves. You will likely have no desire to control experiences and outcomes that protect what has already been created in your life.

Our I AM selves show up as unconditional love. The virtues of a joyful life will make living in harmony with Source, such as loving your neighbor as yourself real. There are many verses in the Bible that state treating others as you would want to be treated or to love your neighbor as yourself is proof positive you've arrived at a point of unconditional love. Loving thy neighbor encompasses all the other directives of becoming a spiritual being because if you love thy neighbor as thyself you are in accord with the Divine, or what is called oneness today. If there is pushback at this point, you'll be able to see how much further you have to go on the path to unconditional love. As you continue to open up to being loved, the path becomes clearer. The truth is, that to love your neighbor as yourself means you've loved yourself above all outcomes.

One of the reasons why there is so much hurt and pain in the world is because on the human plane, we treat each other exactly how we see and feel about ourselves—inadequate. And as we know, "hurt people, hurt people" resulting in a world in a perpetual state of hurt. The hurt and pain we hold on to is a direct reflection of the hurt and pain we've been exposed to, what we see on the news, in our communities, in relationships, and in our lives. If we don't love ourselves, these conditions make it challenging to treat people as we want to be treated. If we are spiritually incomplete we will do things to get attention or bring temporary "feel good" solutions, always seeking fulfillment and love from something or someone outside of ourselves. This potentially leading down the road of wanting to escape life as we know it. Remaining detached from all swirling around us that is spiritually, psychologically, and emotionally destructive is spiritual maturity.

The path to unconditional love is always internal and cannot be found in the outer world. It is the shedding of hurt and pain. It is in releasing the stories our minds created in childhood that allows us the freedom to be who we are and therefore why we are. Carrying the heavy load of our ego selves filled with conditions and judgment into our present lives is what keeps us bound to pain and hurt.

In the ego-bound Western world, even after our basic needs of survival are met, we tend to live thinking our professional titles, material possessions, looks, or financial status are what define our self-worth. These metrics are false narratives that keep people in survival mode. The "I think my way is better than your way" that now permeates most cultures, re-enforces ego and is all too clearly seen in the atrocities the world is experiencing. I was watching an interview recently and the commentary was about how Korean and Chinese cultures are not the same. Which, given their history is accurate, but the thing that had me on pause was that one of the interviewees said, "We still don't even like each other." I don't know why I was surprised because the same sentiments are repeated over and over: France and Germany; Israel and Palestine; England and France, and just about every country has conflict with another. It is more than evident here in the United States that we treat each other poorly in general, always fighting for acceptance in terms of race, ethnicity, wealth, status, sexuality, and religious or non-religious preferences. Each story of claiming one-upmanship may be different, but the result is the same. We are all divided by judgment, opinions, and cultural or religious separation. It always amazes me how the same patterns of existence show up everywhere, especially given we all live here, sharing this planet during our existence. Culture, language, and our differences are opportunities to expand our understanding and should be unifiers affirming of loving presence, rather than separators.

The spiritual world is in juxtaposition to this prevailing behavior. From the position of loving unconditionally everything perceived for yourself and others is generating and returning the goodwill of your heart. Other people receiving your goodwill and paying it forward will truly step into the realm of the ultimate connection our souls crave. Once Faith, Hope, and Love become a part of spiritual practices there is an awareness of what you see, how you feel, and where you are connected or disconnected to oneness—the expanding love that is always within. Fully aware that the power of change is in your hands, your authentic self will start to awaken the hearts of others not by force but by example, leading to what could be a planetary commission: a reconciliation of the human and spiritual planes.

To experience a Glorious Arising, new ways of seeing, feeling, and believing, will ask us to accept the notion of being a part of everything and all things; to suspend disbelief, and to surrender to the wonders of universal connectedness. On the way to being, there is much to be mastered. The beautiful thing about this; you are already in the experience of mastering yourself; loving yourself in ways that never diminish your worth, and fulfilling and embracing all of you with unconditional love. Extend that love to others and they will extend it yet to others. The healing of the world lies in self-love. An inward journey of love of self, others and the divine is the full expression of self-love.

On this path, if chosen, there are three stages of a return to innocence: Faith Hope, and Love. You can use the information presented in this section of the book as a guide, a teacher of sorts to help you on your inward journey of returning to self. Self-awareness through observation and recognition of what you see and how you feel will be followed by full acceptance and surrender. A belief in your true nature leads to the ultimate freedom you seek. It's not a 1, 2, 3, and done scenario, because it is all happening simultaneously, all the time, and all around.

When there is nothing left lingering in your past, what you will carry into your future will be the ability to fully live in the present in peace, joy, love, and community.

For many like me, the past might have included fear, ridicule, judgment, abuse in any form, and a strong desire to fit into what society prescribes as normal. It is a heavy load to carry. A life of "trauma" teaches us how to don the masks that protect us from further damage. Coping with damage might take the form of overpleasing, over-giving, over-tolerating, over-compensating, lashing out, withdrawing, aggression, or the myriad other ways we batter our self-esteem in a bid to self-protect, including shutting down or clamming up to handle the fears that threaten. Depending on the severity of the hurt, we can find ourselves in rigid armor we oftentimes don't realize we are wearing. The mask also feeds into the illusion of separation from self and everything around us, yet masquerades as a critical judgment of ourselves and others, and placing conditions and expectations on each other's behaviors. These unconscious behaviors could give someone struggling with confidence and self-esteem issues more reasons to go further into hiding.

When one day the burden becomes too much we are forced to make a choice. At the point of no return, thrown into a battle of will and total chaos, the soul seeks a way to be remembered…to either awaken fully or remain dormant. This is usually the impetus for most of us to move toward a spiritual awakening. Simply put, as Fannie Lou Hamer said, "I am sick and tired of being sick and tired."

Below Are The Lessons I Wish To Share With You, And How These Lessons Have Helped Me To Reach The Person I Truly AM. I Hope They Help You.

The Lessons:
Nothing New Under the Sun

The earth is 4.543 billion years old. Religious doctrines as we know them today, date back approximately 3,000-6,000 years. So, spiritual teaching is not something pulled out of a hat in this century, but rather time-tested observations and practices of "God"—realized beings who came before us. Five hundred years before the birth of Jesus, a Chinese man by the name of Lao-tzu documented *The Tao,* which in Chinese means path. Many regard this seminal work as the ultimate explanation of the nature of existence. The text gives insight into what a balanced, moral, spiritual, world always working for the good of humanity might look like. Simply put, all the teachings can be distilled into one sentence: Humanity flourishes when aligned with the underlying force that governs everything and cannot be explained fully. In a world that subordinates nature and does not go with the flow of the cosmos, chaos of mind, body, and spirit is the outcome. Many things in the "world" may satisfy the mind and body but nothing in this "world' can satisfy our soul, except living in our true nature of love, joy, peace, patience, kindness, goodness, faithfulness, gentleness, and self-awareness. These are things that cannot be bought or sold. They are within. I used to get frustrated with people telling me I'd find myself within because I didn't know what that meant, nor had a clue how to find it. What they didn't tell me was that all I sought was already within me but disconnected from Source. I was only able to see the outside of me.

As shared in my story, I was forever seeking love from my family, friends, and lovers; affirming my self-worth based on their opinions, my title, role, and status. As far up the ladder as I'd climbed I never felt satisfied, peaceful, or successful. I couldn't get enough of what connected me to the wonders, surprises, mystery and beauty life can bring. Until I began to embrace the lessons of Faith, Hope, and Love, I was unable to access the inward journey that connected me to what is real; the love that will always and forever connect me to the Creator and myself as a fully realized being, and the Holy Spirit, aka the Father, the Son, and the Holy Spirit—the I AM.

YHWH, the Hebrew name for God translates into English to the I AM and in Christian texts to The Holy Spirit, the connective thread within. Seeking a path back to self, and to the remembrance of who we truly are can be daunting in the limiting world. When stuck in our growth, our souls nudge, asking us to surrender what we are holding on to and desiring that we rise up and show that there is more to the world than we know or see with human eyes. Reconnecting your thread to I AM, gives everything in your world its purpose. The interdependence of one on the other is where eternity resides.

Three times the teachings of Faith, Hope, and Love were presented to me outside of the Bible. At *Landmark*, Rythmia Life Center, and through *The Jeshua Code*. The first two experiences I did not make the connection between the teachings of Faith, Hope, and Love for me. It wasn't until I read the *Jeshua Code* by James F. Twyman that it all came together. The funny thing is, I had begun ending my correspondence with the words, *Faith, Hope, Love* in 2008, one year before my son was born, but it wasn't until 2023 that I finally understood I have been on my remembrance journey for seventeen years, beginning at age twenty-eight, and still going.

As I travel my path, I meet more and more people searching for meaning in their lives. There is, I believe, a rise in the number of people seeking to escape, what Henry Thoreau in *Walden* states as, "lives of quiet desperation." By this, he meant the unrest we experience when we lead shallow, inauthentic lives dominated in the pursuit of wealth, competition for success, or relief from man-induced struggles for survival. When success is measured against milestones such as money and "other people's success," and when we succumb to the allure of external fulfillment as the way to achieve happiness, the thing that often awaits us is quiet desperation. Believing too, that external validations are the answer to our inner unrest, looking everywhere, except inward, for acceptance, love, happiness, and peace, lands us in the very same spot—quiet desperation.

On my trek, I came to understand ego always surrenders to the "if only" question: If only I had more power, money, a vacation home, a private jet, the perfect wife, or husband, and it requires more, more, more. Unfortunately, this leads to a vicious cycle that often leaves us spent and in total burnout. Many will stay on the hamster wheel, controlled by the ego. The problem with the ego though, is it's insatiable, and the effects of the elation it delivers are fleeting. It is the ego's limiting beliefs of doubts, erroneous perceptions, illusions, and disillusionment that can lead us to either an awakening or to our possible demise.

In the logical, illusionary world, our fears keep us striving to conform to societal standards that are increasingly insurmountable and often unreasonable. Being asked to conform to the status quo, not only completely ignores our dreams and desires, but ignores the innate you who knows that even with imperfections, there is no one on this planet better at being you than you. Your journey is a singular one and it's what's necessary for your soul to rejoin and add value to the collective consciousness.

We don't have to look far to see herd mentality in action. It is all around us in business, in sports and entertainment; and even in church. A society built on competition is adept at pitting one against the other and discarding those who fall by the wayside. Trying to fit in has limited freedoms which cause health and wellness issues. Tapping into the universal consciousness means leaving the robotic life behind and fully stepping into the realm of finding your true self. An awakening is available to everyone because it is the consciousness of yours' and the universal soul. And here is the beautiful thing about this consciousness….a new beginning is totally in your hands simply because it's your belief—a mindset that you are the I AM <u>that</u> I AM. Discovering you are the I AM lies in shifting behaviors and in believing and embracing the tenets of a spiritual life. You can truly start today.

Spiritual suffering is signaled by the unrest of the soul in its relentless pursuit for authenticity and shows up as a longing for something else that cannot be ignored. It is a sensing from the higher self that there is more to life than you are experiencing, even with all the trappings of a successful life. The signals our intuition receives from the spiritual world to which it is inextricably linked, is that our physical and emotional self is simply a messenger, a trusted or unreliable companion for our higher self. The soul's longing is what we call first nature, a yearning of the soul to get back to its remembered state within us. It's an invitation to look inward so life can reveal its true essence. It's our singular purpose to return to innocence. It is a clarion call for reflection.

As I grew past therapy, past shedding shame and blame, and grew into self-awareness, I understood fully what being in the eye of the storm meant. I was at the center of a difficult, stressful, and trying time in my life surrounded by furious and lashing winds. There was only one thing I could do. Strengthen my faith and conviction to weather the storm. For me, that meant going back to my spiritual foundation. I am not Bible-thumping nor am I preaching to convert others to Christianity. I don't believe there is only one path or belief to God. The truth is there are many traditions and beliefs, be they religious or otherwise, that can connect us, and I have obtained knowledge from many of them. The one I feel most connected to stems from walking in the path of Jesus's teachings. Still, I used to question when the Bible said, "I AM the way the truth, and the life, no one gets to the Father except through me," John 14:6. That was until I understood the path Jesus set, was shaped by the familiar saying, "do as I say not as I do." This means don't imitate my behavior but obey my instructions. Find your way but do as instructed. It is only in the doing so that being a true follower can discern their unique path. I laugh here because I used to say to my kids stop leaving glasses in your room.

One day I was cleaning up my room and became aware of all the glasses I was removing. Needless to say, I stopped telling my children to stop. They being sponges were simply mimicking what I did. It is in the doing that we walk our paths not in the saying but in action. It always amazes me how things unfold at deeper and deeper levels of knowledge when we act. For me, to be a follower of someone or something like a religious or spiritual tradition, I have to feel at a deep level that what is being taught (doing) is in alignment with what is right for me. For I AM that I AM. The name of God, The I AM should be held in high esteem and not bantered around or casually used the way it is today. When this name was said, in biblical times, Jesus did not use it casually or as a singular truth about himself but rather he said it as THE DIVINE CREATRIX or God of all, every self—the collective.

Delving deeper into the faith I was raised with, I began paying more attention to my mom's relentless commitment to her faith as a Christian. She would sit with the Bible on her lap and pray for hours on end that things would shift and change in her marriage and her life, never for one moment losing hope. Despite her limitations, Mom kept working, kept moving forward, and kept striving. She remained centered and consistent, not allowing her circumstances, health, or relationship challenges to derail her as she worked alongside my dad to provide for all of us. Being the forthright person she is, mom never hid how challenging life was for her, but her perseverance and her ability to keep moving forward was incredible for me and in hindsight meant she had tapped into an indestructible faith.

I also began appreciating that it was actually my mom who shaped and influenced a huge part of my life. I'd learned from her never to give up, that there's nothing I cannot accomplish, and that faith can move mountains if those mountains are to be moved. From a young age I observed my parents' relentlessness inside of me, and their strength of character and perseverance today is my inheritance. While my mom showed me the driving passion to live graciously, my dad taught me something as valuable…the value of observation. And that was where I was at that point in my life. In a state of observation.

Like a wound of the physical body seeks healing, a wounded or tortured consciousness is a signal from the soul that it wants to tap into its Divine Matrix. Some will choose, through sheer will of survival to answer the call while others may not. Healing and repairing a wounded consciousness is an ongoing process with many stops and starts. The resurrection journey requires suspension of belief in almost everything you might have held as true, and a knowing and an appreciation that there is no magic elixir for immediate healing.

Overcoming the Stories, We Tell Ourselves

Learning I carried a victim mentality and that I was afraid to love myself and others was the most difficult part of the journey for me. But it was exactly the reason I had opened the door to my healing. A forest burst into spontaneous combustion to clear the way for new growth, so too my soul's battle cry had bust through my victim mentality and rebelled. The soul's journey of returning to itself is instinctual and it will rise up when it feels it's time for your betterment. I listened and I followed. Recognizing my unique purpose in this lifetime was in being able to design the life I loved and wanted, to do that. I had to get past the barriers that kept me rooted.

Don't Bear the Victim Mentality

Suffering is an outcome of control, either from what I am doing to myself or someone else's bid to control me, themselves, and/ or what's around them. So, essentially humans are creating their own suffering. In The Gnostic Gospel *Mary {Magdalene,}* there is a conversation between Jesus and Mary Magdalene that clearly states that what we experience in the world is the result of our own actions and that reuniting our nature with its roots, gives us ears to hear the instructions of reuniting to Source, which is not only possible but desired.

MM: 13. What is the sin of the world?"
The Teacher answered: 15 "There is no sin. 16: It is you who make sin exist, 17: when you act according to the habits 18: of your corrupted nature; 19: this is where sin lies. 20 This is why the Good has come into your midst. 21: It acts together with the elements of your nature 22: to reunite it with its roots." 23: Then he continued: 24: "This is why you become sick, 25: and why you die: 26: it is the result of your actions; 27: what you do takes you further away. 28:

The misconception that suffering is a punishment is incorrect. Suffering will always exist in the world as long as there is control but suffering holds knowledge and choices. The cross we bear depends on these sufferings and is actually what leads to our resurrection journey; it is some form of suffering in our physical and spiritual being. It is a state where we feel like a victim to something or someone. To unearth the hidden gems of our soul requires peeling away the morass gathered from ego-driven behaviors.

Spiritual suffering is as real as physical suffering. It is what made me, at the heights of my career, walk away from the prestige, the money, and the influence I wielded for twenty-five years and leave the table I fought so hard to get to. For me, the predominant cross I chose to bear was the cross of family. For a long time, I felt responsible for my family's financial well-being, especially my parents. Why? Well, that is two-fold. Mamma Annie's drive to move her family out of poverty, and her control over my dad who to her represented the person to carry the baton further down the road, set in motion financial success as a goal to attain. In our succession line, the next person to be passed the baton was the 'additive' me. When I did the things my parents (mostly my father) and great-grandmother valued, I felt loved. In the story, I told myself the reward for lifting the family up, was to be valued. Telling myself this, I over-indexed on behaviors leading to me in service to everyone else, which in my case as CEO of our company, was to protect and expand on the wealth my father created. Who asked me to do this? Me! No one asked me to do so…but since I had assumed the role of caregiver and was really good at it, everyone began to believe it was my responsibility to safeguard the family, including our financial well-being. On occasion, people would ask, who put you in charge? My answer was always *humm*, my dad.

The truth is I can never be responsible for anyone else's life, only mine. I can help other people. I can provide resources to support them, but I'm not responsible for anyone else's feelings, success, or failure. I am not even responsible for my children, rather I serve as a steward and example. They are not me and their journey in this life will be uniquely theirs. I am here to love, to lead with love, to be the love that always is and always will be. I can guide and lead my children and others, provide support, and ask questions but ultimately their actions are theirs. If I am concerned about their actions, I get quiet, sit still, and pray with the certainty that whatever they experience is conspiring for their higher good. I share wisdom and examples and sometimes offer advice, but at the end of the day, what they choose to do with it is their choice. These are the things I do. I had to leave behind that idea as giving all of me was how I'd anchored my self-worth. Now I know the moment I take on the responsibility of someone else, it becomes a burden and suffering. The moment I attempt to take on the burden of pleasing people and trying to make them happy, I quickly shut it down. As I am constantly moving through my spiritual practice, I check myself against this concept. From my new point of view, I can turn these burdens and crosses over to Source. I can stand in uncertainty and still be certain at the same time; I can stand in fear and still be fearless. I can welcome the peaks and valleys, and I can understand the impermanence of all these emotions in the realm of universal truth. Having the tools to identify the cross I should not have to bear is to stand in the truth of who I AM.

The best way for me to become a part of anyone's journey, including my own, is to be myself and fully realize my true nature. Claiming all that I am as I AM displaces my victim's "empty glass" story. For me, that is Faith, Hope, and Love in practice. Unfortunately, the crosses we bear are not habits that will go away easily because that's how our earthly world is built. We all take up a cross for something. Our prevailing world views have created outcomes of being responsible for a lot of angst, jealousy, bitterness, I am better than you mindset, competition, anger, entitlement, self-deprecation, fear; and the list goes on. When options are exhausted, to find peace in the outer world the crosses we bear can be the catalyst that forces us to look inward. To discover how to return to love cannot be explained using the logical mind. It will be futile because spiritual awakening does not fall into the realm of logic.

In my belief of being a victim, I was drawing to myself situations and exhibiting behaviors that continued to make me a victim. Playing the victim was not serving me or my family in any way. Staying constant in my joy, regardless of what was happening around me…would become my challenge. At first, I was still trapped in a victim's loop and over and over again falling into the same pit much like Bill Murphy in the movie *Ground Hog's Day* who kept reliving Feb 2nd. The energy of someone else was controlling me. Simply put, I was stuck, but now I was in a place of observation rather than reaction. Observation acts like the compass charting a ship's course. Understanding what's needed to get from where you are to where you want to go, asks you to become an observer of your life.

Being fully aware of my triggers and touch points both on the inside and out, helped me build a roadmap and blueprint to the life I desired. It is rewarding yet challenging work to create the beauty inside to match the outside, but step by step, if there is a desire, it can be attained. What I hadn't realized was that even when feeling stuck in familiar ways, by being still I could raise my vibrational level and in so doing, became more aware of my predilections. I am a porous, feeling person and hard and jagged-edged energy interrupts my flow. Learning I am the one creating all the negative and positive energy in my life, body, and mind, and that the energy I release controls the quality of my life, was eye-opening. Identifying limiting beliefs and stagnant energy showing up as pain, opened me up to my spiritual growth.

If we dare to look at our lives we'll see most of the crosses we bear are self-imposed. They are our reactions to external forces impacting our lives daily. Don't be afraid to ask yourself what you feel responsible for, then examine it and see if it is really your cross to bear. Most of the time you'll see it is not and you've taken on the mantel of a view that is not God's intent. Through self-love, and despite the fears rooted in you, a path will open up for you to seek and fulfill the true essence of who you are meant to be. When the ego-bound world has failed you is the most likely time a Glorious Arising will occur.

It Is So If You Think It Is So.
The Glass: Empty, Half-full, Full

Imagine before you three clear glasses. One is empty, one is half-full, and one is full. Now shine a prism light into the glasses. What do you see? The glass is always full! The glass-full-empty analogy is all about perception and judgment. How do you see the world? Your life? Is your glass empty, half full, or full? Whatever you believe perceptually, the reality is, that the glass is never empty. If there is no liquid in the glass, the glass is filled with air. If you add liquid halfway, the glass is filled with half liquid and half air, if you fill the glass all the way to the brim, the air is fully displaced, and the glass is filled with liquid. This is simply a displacement and replacement concept. The state of what fills the glass has changed, but the glass itself has not. It is simply a vessel that holds what's in it.

In our cognitive world, we have been taught to look through the lens of empty, half-full, and full. In the spiritual world, this concept does not exist. The air, though invisible to the naked eye in the cognitive world, is a living matter. It is after all what sustains us as we breathe in oxygen from an invisible source. How can we begin to think it is empty? The vibrational frequency of air may be different from the water you poured into the glass, but both frequencies are important to us as humans. Air, water, and light are all part of the living universal continuum.

If you put white light through a prism it will split into all the colors of the rainbow, but you cannot see it unless it passes through a refracting medium…like a rainbow does through clouds. In the example of shining a light through the glass, now imagine our lives in the same state, empty, half-full, and full to overflowing. The light we shine to see the state of the glasses' fullness, is the same as the love we pour into ourselves. If there is no love poured into our glass, we are in a constant state of fear…which is a masterful and powerful motivator of survival and the access point of our ability to live into love. What's real is, that our physical body, like the glass, is a vessel of possibilities, and its state depends on perception, judgment, faith, hope, and love. This should suggest wholeness is our state of being but if we want to experience a different state of being, we can pour whatever we want into our vessel.

If your glass is "completely empty" because it is holding on to fear, hate, anger, self-hatred, etc., to change its state means pouring a different potential into the vessel. If your glass is "completely full it's because it is holding love, connections, joy, and peace that surpasses understanding, you are living as a clear channel of light that passes through every cell in your body and shines bright all around and within you. What potential do you want to pour into yourself? What potential do you want to pour into your half-empty glass? Endless possibilities? If so, the displacement of the "empty" glass has now been filled with a new perspective buoyed by Faith, Hope, and Love. To begin the journey inside will ask you to no longer worry about what the world thinks, but what you think; what you choose to create within and for yourself. It does not matter that you as your vessel is full, half-full, or empty, what matters is that you fill yourself up with love After all, it is your glass from which you will drink.

Lack of Awareness or Awareness?

With so many worldly distractions and choices, a person in denial can distract themself with cravings and addictions for a long time. When they become aware of the need to change, an examination of what in life has served their purpose and what has not will be pursued. It'll be like Spring cleaning…and they get to decide what stays and what goes. Awareness is a key that opens the lock to change.

When I walk through life now, I am aware. I ask myself, what am I holding on to that holds me back from what I want for myself. Which illusion am I wedded to? With my spiritual toolbox wide open I am aware that the only thing God has ever asked me to do is to love as myself; to live as myself; to give as myself; to receive as myself what is mine; and to trust everyone else walking their path will come face-to-face with themself. And the only way to do this is if I truly love myself unconditionally. I am constantly revisiting my spiritual path as acumen does not come from a one-and-done effort but from constant reiteration, practice, fine-tuning, and understanding. Because the world of Source is dynamic, as I move further and further down the path of enlightenment, I have come to realize that true enlightenment and awareness are the ability to see, feel, and discern everything I have created, deciding what's reality and what's illusion. As the master creator of what I see, feel, and love about myself and others I can move further along my path to unconditional love. Awareness, observation, acceptance, and claiming I AM bring me to the door of unconditional love. I just now have to embrace it.

Even to this day, I am constantly working on my remembrance journey. I check in on my awareness as I am still moving through my journey of expanding my love. Every time I re-walk the experience, I'm shown something new about what I've created for myself. I am also able to give myself grace, compassion, and love for what I did not know in my past behavior. In my practices and reviews, if something gives me pause, this new knowledge allows me to expand my love of self and others. If I am not yet showing up in the world how I want to be and am feeling disconnected from myself, or from loving myself, I know there is still a distance to go to fully integrate Source. Being aware of my limitations, when I'm claiming something good, such as generosity, depth of understanding, empathy, compassion, joy, and love, I check to make sure I am in alignment with spirit. Agape love—unconditional love does not evoke fear. Aware and comforted by the fact that even though I may feel disconnected, in reality, I know I am always connected to Source, and that any sense of disconnection in the way I see and feel is under my control. I now have the chance to shift how I feel about 'it.' As I recognize I'm holding myself back from all that I have been created to be, I can pour every ounce of love I can muster into claiming the love that is, I AM. When the Universe is mirroring my hopes and dreams and it is not as I see, it will ask me to expand my view of the Divine— the divine, not human truth.

It is in the moment that I embrace everything I see and feel—every emotion, including fear, anger, and pain, every thought, every action, everything about myself and others without conditions, expectations, or judgment and I can be with it/ them as they are—that is the point of loving bigger than your fears.

Surrender Judgment … It Is A Peak Experience.

Judgment does not work in a spiritual world because God is love and love has no judgment. Agape love, bigger than all other loves, neutralizes all judgment and conditions and is the full acceptance of all that is, as it is. If I'm truly going to be that love, I'm going to stand in it without exception and I'm going to let the wave of how I feel go through the peaks and the valleys of those moments as they are.

In divine reality, to be the architect of a life desired and filled with all you want it to be, surrender is essential. As you oscillate between resurrection and reality, release judgment from the stories you tell yourself and the meaning of what has happened, is happening, or will happen. Letting go of what does not promote your greatest good ushers in the next and ultimate level of "knowing. "Agape love then becomes completion and is absolute. That means it has only one side.

Very few things in life are one-sided. Two hands, two nostrils, two feet, two eyes, two ears, two animals of every kind in Noah's Ark, two sides of a coin, the other side of the argument, of love, and hate, happy and sad. Why? Because knowing the existence of both and seeing and feeling how duality leads to the very same place, I've learned to see and feel life the way it truly is. I recognize duality reveals opposites that are complements of each other and that the duality of everything is the oneness of all there is. When I think of hot and cold I experience different temperatures, yet they are both temperatures. If I focus on the feeling of either hot or cold or hot and cold, they are still both temperatures.

When I was just learning this concept in my spiritual practice my marriage was ending. I was determined to show my husband, Paul, unconditional love no matter the conflict between us. It was either unconditional love or walking through the valleys of uncontrolled anger for an hour at a time. That was too exhausting, and it was the complete opposite of who I wanted to be and how I wanted to feel. I wanted to model this as an example for my children of what love looks like for a family that is nontraditional in many ways yet remains a family. No judgment meant having grace and compassion and the ability to look at both sides of a story. I was able to own my responsibility for the ending of my marriage and still know my marriage would end. That's just the nature of standing in the duality of no judgment. There are things that die and should. In letting go of things for your spiritual growth relationships will be left; there are people who you will unfollow, and there are things to avoid at all costs as they conflict with your flow. Yet you can still stand in no judgment while standing in God's love. Knowing choices are necessary allows you to thrive as yourself. This opens up the ability to create new possibilities in how love can work within relationships with yourself and others.

Part of the remembrance journey is going through peaks and valleys. Wherever you are, just stand in it. Stand in the experience and try to come through on the other side of those emotions with a sense of detachment. For me, detachment means I feel what I feel and that's it. I do not act on those feelings. When I tap into love, I experience beauty, and pleasure radiates throughout my body because I am no longer stifling or denying what I feel. I am witnessing rather than acting on feelings. Doing so reinforces your journey and does not detract from or diminish the power of God in you. In the valley, you may be fully immersed in your pain while at the peak you are a channel of God's love.

One of the biggest lessons Jesus taught me was the disempowerment of enabling others. If my judgment is, that you are incapable, I might do several things, one of which is not staying in my true self as I AM.

My I AM self does not want to do things for people just because I can. Instead, my I AM self deeply wishes people are capable of learning what they can do for themselves. My role is to teach them how to do so. I don't want to replace their "inability" to do, with my ego-driven acumen and superior know-how. I want to, like in the Bible story, teach people how to fish so they can be self-sustaining.

CHAPTER TEN

THE PRINCIPLES OF THE EMISSARY WHEEL A SPIRITUAL TOOL AS YOU JOURNEY ON THE PATH TO A GLORIOUS ARISING.

☥

I had met the idea of Faith, Hope, and Love as keys to opening my spiritual door along the way, but it wasn't until I happened upon the Emissary Wheel that I was able to transform the way I integrated its teachings of what I saw, felt, and loved into my life. When the Emissary Wheel, another master teacher tool came into my life, I went from seeing my healing process as something I was running away from to inviting healing in. It was then that I realized, that the Emissary Wheel principles were the very ones I have been experiencing, but without awareness, observation, or acceptance of the truth I was unable to claim them. I began living its principles in earnest, sometimes walking, crawling, or running at full speed toward my healing journey. Throughout my journey, I carried the narrative that everything was painful and hard. In doing so, I was often making my healing journey harder to walk through. Probably because I was brought up witnessing my mom living in pain and the many missed opportunities we experienced to grow within McDonald's without fighting for our success, I saw success as a hard-won battle.

To this day my family fights for parity, equity, and the ability to create prosperity for people of color, especially African Americans. It is and has always been, a narrative of struggle and survival to get ahead for us, and that's the way I saw life—through the lens that life was going to be hard and painful. I was going to have to work twice as hard to get half as much and I carried my entire race on my shoulders. These stories and narratives that were a part of my upbringing also became a part of my way of being. Why wouldn't any journey I undertake not be hard? It wasn't until the Emissary Wheel and its teachings of the twelve principles that I realized each of us can create our healing experience in a way that is not a made up story or scary.

Following and learning about these principles made it easier to recognize within myself the virtues that existed and I was able to heal from a place of creation filled with love and joy instead of the hell I'd created in my mind. With the new knowledge, I could do so with grace, ease, and love, and a lot of times I derived great pleasure from the new ways I was able to see and create. If a new way of seeing and creating is what you want, the Emissary Wheel could be a place to start.

The Principles of the Emissary Wheel, A Spiritual Tool as You Journey on the Path to A Glorious Arising.

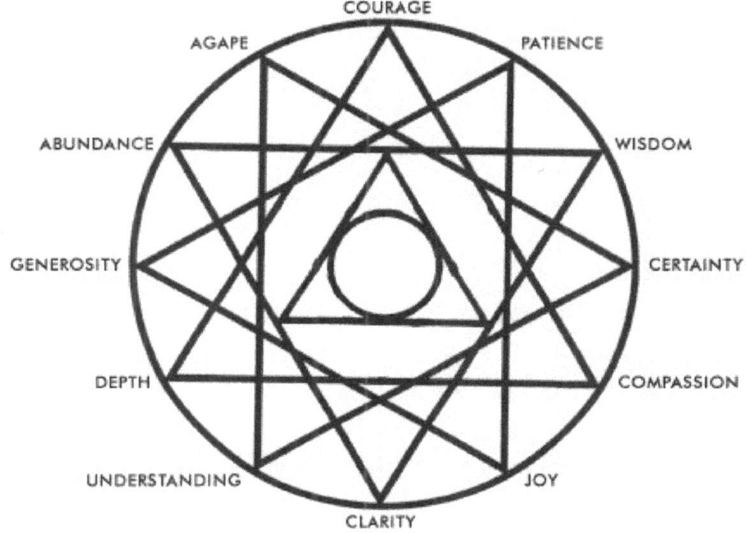

Permission to Reprint granted.

In my struggles with my remembrance journey, I was having a conflict between my spiritual walk and the teachings of Christianity. I prayed for help and was led to a book, the *Jeshua Code*, which is based on the Emissary Wheel and uses the tenets of Faith, Hope, and Love to illuminate. It opened my mind to who I was, who I desired to be, and who I AM. Awakening, my heart, and my soul began to resonate with where I was at any moment in time.

The Emissary Wheel contains profound information that seeds the truth of oneself and starts to activate the code within as one moves toward spiritual awakening. Looking at the Emissary Wheel, you'll see the interconnectedness of the points leading to spiritual transformation. It seemingly goes in clockwise order from Courage to Agape, but it is really the interconnectedness of each point to the other, and the interaction and overlapping of all points on the circle that unlocks the code that is unique for you—all leading toward your inner peace, joy, and love.

As I moved through using the Emissary Wheel in my spiritual transformation, I tried to frame the understanding and the context of my story, through the lenses of Faith, Hope, and Love, and how they could help me navigate my situation. Before I discuss this however, let me once again define Story, Faith, Hope, and Love. Story is the narrative we tell ourselves about the experiences we are having. Faith is an illumination of the mind. The ability to see what was unseen before. Hope is the awakening of the heart; it's our feelings, and Love is the full acceptance and claiming of what you see and how you feel about what you see and feel. Love—oneness—is the full acceptance of self, others and all there is. It is not just a feeling or an emotion; it is all you see, all you feel, and all you are. With or without your knowledge, love still exists, because the existence of love is the absolute of I AM. That is why love is all there is and all there is, is love In other words, love is the realized soul where you can see a situation in its entirety. To master your journey, below are some of the tenets of the Emissary Wheel that could be helpful.

The Emissary Wheel has all the qualities in the human plane that embodies I AM. In the spiritual plane, the Emissary Wheel moves dynamically to a place where you see, feel, and experience God. As scripture states, "he who perceives me everywhere and beholds everything in ME never loses sight of ME. Nor do I ever lose sight of him." From the Bhagavad Gita, this scripture means you will always see yourself as the divine being you are. Once you have seen it for yourself, that what is true for you is true for everyone, you'll understand that not everyone sees what you see so there can be no right or wrong experience. It just is. From here on, your enlightened journey becomes your reality and truth, informing how you got here and why what you have experienced was needed for the ultimate discovery of who you are—a soul without conditions, expectations, or judgments of yourself and others.

Every principle point on the Emissary Wheel stands on its own and interacts and builds on each other. **Courage plus Patience** equals **Wisdom; Certainty plus Compassion** equals Joy; **Clarity plus Understanding** equals Depth; Generosity plus **Abundance** equals Agape.

As you stare at the wheel you come to realize that living in the eye, the triangle with the circle within, is the place to be because it is the touchpoint of all the principles where love, joy, peace, patience, kindness, goodness, faithfulness, and self-control live. Just like living in the eye of a swirling storm, the safest place to be is in the eye of the Emissary Wheel.

We know there will always be storms in our lives. There will be sunny days, wintery days, and many in between. Yet you and only you, with divine love shining through, can keep your peace. When you look up at a raging storm, it takes courage to see through the mess surrounding you and to be able to stand in your truth, see reality, and exercise patience for yourself and others as each is traveling their path. However, as you look up and through the eye of the storm another phenomenon is observed—a clear view of the blue sky peeking through and the "absolute knowing" that with patience, this too shall pass. Wisdom is the outcome of the combination of **Courage and Patience.** Know this too, being alone in the eye of the storm affords a patience that from a divine perspective mimics all nature.

The outcome of **Courage and Patience** is that you see and feel the chaos but you are no longer being ruled by emotions but rather gaining wisdom. The acceptance of outcomes lands you at a point of certainty which in turn leads to the choices you make about what the next steps on the path will be. Because you have begun to follow only your path as the divine being you are, not the path others create for you, you know you are meant to be here. Your understanding of your God-Self deepens.

Clarity and Understanding lead to depth. Depth comes from seeing, feeling, and embracing what was hidden from view before. Depth of connection to all things, your soul spirit, and body allows the appreciation that everything is one, and attachments to the past, while sometimes still hard to let go of, have no meaning except those you give it. In our human plane, the lengths taken to hold on and control things are the reason we are being asked to let go. Letting go gives freedom to create and achieve all you have ever imagined. Depth in the spiritual plane gives access to, and the ability to unlock buried or dormant gifts, just like Jesus did. Depth comes with the understanding of which Tree you are feeding off.

Compassion now comes into play because you've recognized what you didn't know before, and you can forgive yourself and others for having lived in the illusions of what was seen and felt, and the meaning of the stories carried. Now there is no story, only what happened, you're left with compassion for yourself and others. Out of **Certainty and Compassion** comes **joy**. The inner joy has nothing to do with happiness but rather the evanescent and ever-present feeling of YES! The joy of being yourself. Joy leads to an open spirit, one that is generous and kind.

Generosity then, is giving everything, you want for yourself to others. Do unto others as you would have them do unto you. This is all about how we treat each other. The way I want to interact with others is by always looking through the fruits of the spirit: love, joy, peace, patience, kindness, goodness, gentleness, faithfulness, and forbearance; the overarching principles of the Emissary Wheel also known as self-awareness and self-control. Because the universal law states you get what you give, abundance will flow through all you do when in this divine state. Put another way, what you sow is what you reap and you will receive all you are creating for your life. It is therefore important to be absolutely certain about what you claim and create because abundance comes as it is given. Give love, love comes; give hate, and hate is returned.

Knowing that you are divinely generous and abundant leads to **Agape;** the love that is truly unconditional leads to Enlightenment. You are enlightened to what is real and what is an illusion, and you live from the fruits of the spirit. Now you are creating your life, your world, and your relationships, with yourself and others from I AM. All that remains is Faith, Hope, Love and the greatest of these is Love! When you have arrived at this point you'll want to share the "Good News" with others and give what you have to others knowing fully well, that in doing so, you're giving to yourself. And because we are all one, you are giving to the world.

Individual Touchpoints on the Wheel.
Courage.

Courage is the ability to face something you don't want to yet still move towards. In both the physical and spiritual plane, courage is moving us towards change. In the spiritual sense, it is in the releasing of control—the letting go of what you think you wanted, instead of walking confidently into the love of self and the divine essence of your being. The courage to love we speak of here, is the courage to know without fear that you will never be separated from the love that you are. To know that while your body passes on your soul never dies is to accept your everlasting life.

But courage is not a lack of fear. It is a belief that our steps are ordered. It takes courage to do a spiritual walk because you'll be facing things about yourself you might want to resist. You may even lose relationships as you claim your authentic life. But finding courage, as with all of the tenets in the Emissary Wheel, is easier said than done. Once you embrace them, however, they feed upon themselves, building your spiritual muscles in ways you never imagined. Awareness, which we spoke about in its own section, is so important because it is the nourishment courage needs.

When I became aware that in my brother Kyle's eyes, I was stifling him, it was much easier to understand his frustration. My love for him and holding on to him as a bright light in my life was trapping him in my world. With my unblinded eyes, though it frightened me to death, I wanted to find a way to free him. Without being aware, I would not have had the courage to let him go. Taking responsibility for my life meant letting go of the control my expectations created around my relationship with Kyle.

Patience

Patience is referenced in the Bible as be still and knowing I AM God. It is surrendering expectations, delaying gratification, and moving into flow with a certainty that brings you everything you need. "Be still" is not meant to imply without movement. You are the one who decides what to keep and what to discard. What you want to come to you and what you don't. Patience is the ability to pause, rest, and wait for what you acted on and asked for to be delivered right into your direct path. Remember, the invitations of the Universe are always there and patience improves their recognition.

But Patience is a big muscle to build. Things are going to happen that make us impatient. Whatever the cause of the turmoil, as upsetting as it may be, delaying taking action is the kind of tolerance patience needs. Patience requires empathy and the ability to walk in someone else's shoes for a moment in time. To truly see them as they are, not as we want them to be. Patience requires an appreciation of the now and the ability to let life flow.

My appreciation of patience was accidental. It was a breakthrough that happened when what I thought I was doing was withholding and punishing. After Kyle's and my meltdown, I spent days in my garden appreciating the beauty and wonder of the world, yet I was deep in anguish. For three months I cried more tears than there were rivers. I thought I was punishing my offenders by not fixing anything broken. What I didn't know was, those months in my garden were a form of exercising patience. That patience gave me a distant view of my reality. Had I rushed in to fix everything as was expected of me, my life would have floated back to the status quo, and I would have been lost a lot longer in the morass of delusion rather than enter into a dance with the larger forces shaping my life. With me holding out, it forced both my family and me to shift into a new normal. The truth is, I didn't want to go back to the family business. The desire for social status and to stay on the course of ambition to win at all costs was gone. I was being called to do something else.

With the discovery of my path, which was 180 degrees away from McDonald's, there was no way I could return to where I'd been. I had run myself out of time and I needed a new vision. Those few months of faux patience reinforced my courage to step out on faith. When I shared my vision with my family for a series of centers for people to experience 'glorious arisings' for themselves, I was flatly told they would not support it. How dare I jeopardize and gamble the family wealth on such an esoteric and frivolous idea? At that stage of my self-growth, I understood their refusal for what it was...fear of the unknown. To tell you, not only did I have to exercise great patience, but I had to fall face forward into the wisdom of my council. When they say patience is a virtue, it really is.

Wisdom

When you have courage and patience, wisdom is knowing which paths to take. What to say yes to and what to say you are passing on. It is the deep understanding of your inner knowing.

I have always had business wisdom...often called business acumen. The soundness of my actions and decisions added several zeros to my family's bank accounts. Business wisdom was the reason I succeeded at McDonald's when my father put his faith in me. Emotional Wisdom, only acquired through past blunders and challenges, are building block not easy to attain. Understandably, because I had been emotionally shut down for so long, accessing my true emotions was hard for me. It took me many years to come to terms with wisdom and if you ask me today if I have conquered the art of wisdom, I still would not be able to answer. Wisdom requires curiosity and going beyond boundaries. With awareness, regret for me now is nothing but wasted energy unless I use it as a lesson in building wisdom. Wisdom is knowing a mastered mind leads to a mastered life. End of story.

Certainty

Certainty is divine "knowing" that everything is working in order. To have certainty is to know God. Knowing that you are who you are and that your existence is purposeful, its purpose being the discovery of you as you uncover your soul, is a certainty. The fact that you are here when looked at through the lens of certainty and the eyes of love, gives an appreciation of the gift you are to the world. You will always be the gift that keeps giving and gifts will always come back to you.

Certainty is the Holy Grail of belief in an outcome predicted or proven. The sun rises every morning, and the moon every night. That's a certainty. Certainty is absolute. At the point of certainty, we know what we know is true.

Observe the sea and the deserts and realize their importance to our existence. In search of knowledge, it might be good to watch some of the documentaries on the series *Our Planet* to truly appreciate the magnificence of the world at both the macro and micro levels. That our oxygen level is maintained by swirling sand in Africa making its way to the Amazon which in turn releases the oxygen all living things use, and to us humans as the breath of life, is remarkable! It would be impossible not to see the vastness and complexity of a Universe that is deeply interconnected and interdependent.

A 1977 study at the Quantum Physics department at the University of Geneva has proven the theory of entanglement—all particles are connected, and changing the state of one influences the state of the other. You may have heard of the butterfly effect which is a similar chaos theory about cause and effect. Or the saying you reap what you sow. Understanding who we are as humans in the larger context of the Universe and how our actions impact others is an important concept to grasp on the way to awakening. Many ancient civilizations have instinctively known this before modern science and have always worked in harmony with the universe. The Divine, believe it or not, wants interconnection as a means to manage change. Change comes as we move through cycles of high or low vibrational frequencies. The cycle determines the corresponding effects. The wonderful addition to an awakened life is knowing; that is, certainty.

For me, belief in God ordering my steps was a certainty. This meant I could trust the universe and stay 'present' in every moment. Certainty is one of the main cornerstones of spiritual awakening; it is when you can bring out your Bob Marley song and sing at the top of your lungs. "Don't worry about a thing 'cause every little thing is gonna be alright," That's right because the Universe got this.

Compassion

Compassion stems from one's ability to see through the lenses of others while seeing through your own. Compassion is knowing that if you have feelings and a way of seeing things, so do others. It is the realization and appreciation that everyone is having a life experience and being able to share others' vision as well as your own. The fact that you both see a different point of view but can recognize, validate, and support each other's feelings and vision, is compassion. Compassion then is about a shared experience, togetherness.

A great byproduct of my spiritual journey was the ability to see people. I mean really see people. Compassion for me was one of the easier qualities to master. I count it among the highest virtues I value. I experienced compassion one day in school when a nun told me I was going to hell for not believing in the way she interpreted God. The principal, as well as my basketball coach, showed me the kind of understanding, kindness, and compassion that has stayed with me to this day. Being able to wish good and offer kindness when others are in need can go a long way in healing an ailing world.

When I think back on our company, I think a lot of our success was due to our compassion, and likewise, the compassion of our employees. My dad's knack for making people "feel good" about their potential was an act of compassion. The community we served inspired compassion in us. I truly believe our company's culture, values, and leadership centered around compassion. When we hired young workers from our community, trained, supported them, and changed the trajectory of their lives, in my mind it was compassion.

In almost every aspect of life, and in almost every formal and informal world religion, compassion is often high on the list of virtues. We often hear God is benevolent and compassionate and I know it is true. Compassion is a powerful emotion inspiring us to look beyond ourselves and reach out to those in need in ways that improve their lives, mentally, physically, and spiritually. Compassion is the reason for my calling to create Glorious Arising. It is the goodness of the world.

Joy

Joy is finding goodness in all you see, and feel, and recognizing it in others. The feeling of goodness in everything is divine love because it stems from Source. Not every action feels or seems loving, but joy is at the core of what people want, and they are usually the same things: safety, security, acceptance, belonging, success, and finding and discovering themselves. When on a soul walk one is finally able to fully integrate the idea that they had never left themselves, oneness is understood.

It's been a long walk to my joy but I know real joy is possible because I have experienced it. From the outside looking in I should have embodied happiness and be the epitome of joy because I had a lot. Sharing the torture in my soul probably would have made me seem like a spoilt, whining, bratty kid of a family that would have been considered privileged with financial security and enviable opportunities. The beauty of joy is it deletes the "if only" question. If only I wasn't so tall! In a model's world, some might have coveted my 6' 2" height and the model figure I worked hard to keep. When you have reached a level of joy the "what if" question becomes neutralized.

As I previously said, one of the falsehoods we live under in modern times is the belief that life should always be happy and rewarding. Drummed into us early by the happily ever after stories we are told as children, if you have lived long enough, you'll come to understand the impermanence of emotional states. Happiness, like any other emotion, is never a permanent state. Emotions ebb and flow along the spectrum of life, giving us clues as to who we are and the lessons we need to pay attention to, to find our joy.

Where am I on the Joy spectrum today? I'm free. I am no longer influenced by what people think. Not thinking about and not caring what people think is knowing my worth is not defined by them and that includes my family. I admit this is very, very challenging for me, but that I can keep my own counsel is a sign of internal maturity, and for that I am grateful. Now I find, even in the midst of an emotional upheaval, I'm at peace with the decisions I've made about *my* life. It is a peace that brings me real joy, even as tears I cannot fully explain are falling. So, my journey to finding joy has been a really beautiful experience and as I continue to move in the right direction to higher and higher vibrations of joy, I am experiencing a peace, before unknown. Knowing that my joy is not tied to a goal has been freeing.

Clarity

Clarity is seeing the full truth as it exists and being able to discern what's for you and what is not. Clarity of who you are is what makes your creations come into view. Simply put, clarity is seeing what is real, and understanding the distortion and illusion of the narratives created and placed on an experience are harmless.

I am at a point in my life where I understand I am wealth. I am abundance. I am courageous. I am certain. I no longer question God. The work I have to continue to do is around my positioning. Have

I embraced enough of the qualities needed to receive the grace and direction back to a self who remembers?

Clarity is mastering and focusing the mind—blocking out the noise and distortions of daily overstimulation. I can say with a shift in perspective; in changing the way I thought of things; in understanding the why of my challenging journey; in living in the present versus the past; in being unattached to the future; in appreciating the interconnectedness of every living thing; in finding the courage and the wisdom to step out on faith has not only proved liberating but has opened me up to the clarity I need to always be in a position to receive. Training the mind to remain in a state of calm even as the chaos swirls around makes clarity a central pillar of a spiritual journey. Clarity gives us the bandwidth to be mindful by decluttering and cutting through the noise of wasted energy.

Understanding

Understanding human desires is a complex issue. Yet it is understanding that unlocks the doors to internal power, to the mastery of compassion, clarity, and forgiveness. Understanding is when you have attained wisdom—that is comprehension. As we know, many people in the world have comprehension problems so forgiveness will be a necessity in buttressing the world of human desires. Understanding means a deep and meaningful level of knowledge backed by experience and pedagogy. It means curiosity, learning, and the ability to apply knowledge to making sound decisions. Understanding embraces the concept, that every experience and decision we make is 100% our responsibility and determines the outcome of our existence. This is scary. Right? Sometimes what makes it harder to decipher understanding is the inability to tell if someone understands or if they are pretending to understand. Deep understanding gives a level of discernment and allows us to avoid unpleasant situations while honing our ability to support others.

Depth

Depth is a yardstick of growth. Recently I was sitting in a remodled bank branch. There was a booth for high-value clients. Before my new and enlightened journey, I would have made a beeline to the VIP counter that indicated my client status. Instead, I found myself looking at the booth with a...Huh! Huh! Did I need that in the past to validate my life? And now it was just, huh?

That counter represented financial wealth but with new eyes, I understood wealth as so much more than finances. True wealth is five-pronged: social, physical, mental, financial, and most of all the cohesive spiritual wealth that keeps the wheel spinning. This is a hard lesson to grasp for people who have never had wealth and who believe to solve their problems in life all they need is money. People in this position are justified in their thinking for in a capitalist society money makes the world go around. So many attain wealth only to lose it and start over again because at their core, is a limiting mindset.

Because of my parents' upbringing, steeped in a lack mentality, their fear of losing all they have built over fifty years is justified. It falls in the realm of Scarlett O'Hara's Syndrome of "As God is my witness, I will never be hungry again." It is understandable and I have compassion for their feelings of fear and the energy they place on a perceived lack that holds them hostage. Being in a hostage mindset prevents them from seeing possibilities. Facing the demand of running out of time, maybe they feel they are too old to start over. But the truth is they don't have to start over, not in this life, they just have to trust and pass the baton to their children who are more than capable of building the generational wealth they envision. The evidence is clearly on the P/L statements, and it has already been done. The depth of their understanding had been crowded out by lack and it is my great desire that my parents get to a point where they understand the universe is abundant, and they don't have to hold on so tightly to what was but be ready and open to receive God's grace for what could be. It is my desire their fear lessen as they come to appreciate eternity. But the journey is clearly theirs and if it is to happen, I will leave that in God's hand. It's not my cross to bear.

Generosity

Generosity can be misunderstood. It has been used to bilk people out of millions of dollars in the spirit of doing good. Think of all the shenanigans of non-profit organizations that return 80% of giving to themselves through their operational budgets, or how about filling the offering plate of pastors who buy lavish vacation homes and private jets while their congregation struggles with day-to-day living? That kind of generosity is conditional and preys on human frailties.

Spiritual generosity is not about filling the offering plate or giving to unscrupulous organizations. Let me be clear, as a Christian this is not God's intent. The culture of generosity of which I speak is a path to transformation for the seeker who wishes to impact the world and make deep and meaningful connections with humanity. If there is an elixir for life, generosity is it. Scientifically proven is the theory that generosity actually releases the hormone Dopamine in the body. Dopamine makes us feel pleasure, satisfaction, and motivation. Giving produces a natural high and by the equal exchange of giving and receiving in balance, generosity has so many benefits for us as individuals and for the world as a collective. The ultimate generosity exists and is free in a universe that offers rewards beyond our wildest dreams if we only understood how to access the accrued benefits of a true giving spirit.

Abundance

Abundance is a state of mind. Every one of us is probably familiar with the book *As a Man Thinketh*. Its premise is our thoughts create our reality. Thought is energy that can mold our lives to our vision. Transmitted, it joins forces with the energy of the universe to give us what we desire. Cosmic alignment and spiritual acumen mean fully grasping the tenet of abundance to create what you envision.

Along your journey, you have to set intentions. You have to name what it is you want to attract in your life. This dance between the inner and outer self in alignment with the universal source, is what we seek to attain when we set intentions. Embracing the law of attraction by changing the energy field around you brings you closer to your vision.

Here we will come to understand we can have anything our heart desires if we can use the power of the mind to manifest what already exists in our cosmos awaiting our request. A mind mired in limiting beliefs will manifest as a limiting life. The mind in tune with the cosmic energy of abundance will manifest abundance.

When I walked out of Webb Family Enterprises as the CEO, I will tell you, I was scared. No, I was petrified. Petrified I would let my parents down, petrified that I would have no identity, petrified I would never be able to earn my generous income elsewhere ever, and petrified that my life was over at forty-five years old. I wished someone had told me way before I found out that I was the architect of my own life; I would have appreciated it. Imagine how much more I could have accomplished had I embraced a mindset of abundance. I am not talking just about my ability to meet and exceed financial goals but that I could have had my dream of what it is I wanted to share with the world manifested right along with my ability to create financial prowess for our family's company.

When the experience of God's love and the will of cosmic abundance is lacking, creating from a position of lack, fear will always be a life partner, and scarcity a reality. Now I understand I am wealth, and I am abundance, the fear of stepping out on my own has dissipated. And when my family said they would not back my vision for building Glorious Arising Centers I was okay with that because it was already done as I had long named my desire and already knew I was ready to love bigger than my fears. I didn't have to waste precious energy in worry but instead moved toward my limitlessness and to what I hope is the final, yet ever-evolving stage, of my journey. Agape Love.

Agape

Agape is the Greek translation of Love. Ahavah is the Hebrew translation and in Jesus's Aramaic language, Rakhma means love. At the top of the pyramid of self-actualization is Agape love, the total of an awakening with no-hold bars. Agape sits above all other forms of love mentioned in the bible…love of family and friends (philia), romantic love, (eros), self-love (philautic), and is a profound love that transcends. A selfless love passionately committed to the well-being of others, is the love needed to heal the world.

Love though can be another loaded word. It's bandied about, yet we know from past experiences that "love" is given or withheld based on circumstances. My dad and mom loved their children in the way they knew how, and my dad loved my mom in the way he knew how. Yet, my mom's fervent wish to this day is that my dad could love her the way she needs to be loved and his is that she understands his love was in providing an exceptional life for his family, which he did in a magnanimous way. And therein lies the rub. Like everything else love does not come in a one-size-fits-all all. What love is in reality, is ineffable and there are different forms of love. The love I speak of is Agape love. It is not something one says but something one feels when an open mind and heart are free of judgment.

My spiritual group was essential in reminding me what I had forgotten, and most of us forget, we have always come from love. Their help got me back to my awareness of the love that has never left me. Discovering truths, I did not see, feel, or experience in life, with unblinded faith I was led to me loving without conditions, expectations, or judgments. To experience the profound love within that allowed me to be fully in the grace and free, was the ultimate gift from my journey.

To unlock the latent gifts that already existed within; to reconnect a future from a present that healed the past is true freedom. Once free, what is possible is beyond understanding

It may be hard to believe given the despair of the times, an emerging world is on the way. A world of love, connectedness, abundance, and limitlessness is certain. This selfless, unconditional love is not self-seeking, does not dishonor others, keeps no record of right or wrong, is not easy to anger, and is the acknowledgment of the Divine and the highest moral virtue. A pure and conscious love...otherwise known as unconditional love, is the point of true ascension into Agape love. A spiritual event is likely to happen when we return to the perfection of our creator who is perfect, as are we. Agape love includes all the tenets leading up to it and is what transforms an ordinary existence into an extraordinary one fully realized and integrated with Source. When everything is in sync with the cosmos, (the I AM in my case) a Glorious Arising occurs.

As I begin anew and am awakened, I am armed with the knowledge that having unconditional love for myself opens up the space for others to come to the awareness that they are the I AM. As I set out to create what I know is my purpose, I bring all of me to the table. No one has to let me into the room because it is a table of my creation and I invite you all to sit with me. My wish upon which I set my intention is: I wish we could all see how amazing life is when we do it together.

CHAPTER ELEVEN
THE POWER OF I AM

☥

The use of I AM is very powerful, it is the seeding of what you create for yourself. When aware you are an integral part of the universal matrix and that your actions impact and affect all, you have become a co-creator with Source and your behaviors and thoughts influence the reality you experience. It is in this realm of the I AM where you are at a spiritual frequency when the intentions you've set can be created. Every time you use I AM know that you are speaking as your divinity and that everything following is true about yourself. If you think and say, I AM followed by tired, you are creating the being of tired. You are embodying it. I often tell my children and remind myself to use I AM statements with care and intention.

Creation.

Our role in co-creation lies in the understanding of who we are and naming what we claim. Fully understanding that at every moment we are co-creating with the universe is a powerful revelation. In co-creation, we each do our singular part and we need to show up with action to back the dreams and wishes we put out into the universe. Naming what you want to create sets your intention and the law of attraction, the language the universe understands, in motion. With action comes creation. It encompasses all of the principles of the twelve tenets of the Emissary Wheel. These qualities are what allow creation to happen without interference.

The code of creation is in everything. It's why we grow and evolve. When fully allowing creation to happen with set intentions of what you want to create, a shift occurs that opens up the abundance of the world directing your path toward that creation. Just as the seasons have indicators for change, there is a clear order of how creation works. There are three parts of creation: the imaginative cycle, rest, and the unfolding. Creation seemingly comes from a blank slate but like the perception of an empty glass, there are unseen resources embedded from which we can design the life we desire. And if you can imagine it, you can do it.

In every creation story, it always begins with our divinity, then Spirit then humanity. Most things I have created in the past, including my healing journey, began in reverse. I wanted to heal my human self to be worthy of my I AM self while asking the Spirit for help. The moment I say that everything I start, from a business to a relationship, is in motion, my expansion into love always begins with my divinity. My I AM self then asks for guidance and support from Spirit and then I watch as things unfolds and manifests in my humanity.

Cause and Effect.

Awareness that for every action there is a clear, equal, and opposite reaction, becomes a part of our conscious mind. This means thinking before acting. Being deliberate and not impulsive leads to a full understanding of self and therefore the ability to accurately name our desired outcome. Clearly understanding that whatever is put out into the universe will come back to you is beneficial. If the output is negative it will impact your life negatively. Conversely, if it is positive so shall you reap. And because we understand the continuum and connectedness of everything in the universe, we also now understand that through our creation, everything and everyone will be impacted by our singular actions. This is a pivotal point on the awakening journey. This power concept can indeed lead to what was coined by John Randolph Price in 1984 in *The Planetary Commission,* "As you lift up your consciousness and open a channel for the Light from within, you will be doing your part to heal and harmonize the planet. In truth, which is why you are here."

I mentioned earlier that with my change my family also changed. They may not have changed in the way I did, but a shift has definitely occurred. My actions set in motion a response to their actions both on the plus and negative side. Because of my ability to let go, my brother Kyle experienced a freedom unavailable to him before—one that currently has him fighting within himself. Access to feelings and emotions that are too scary to experience bottles up inside him. Because I was not reticent about my faith and my certainty, I was able to pray with my parents around their fear of loss. They in turn were able to, if even for just a moment, recognize the power of letting go and letting God. This is the reason they are believers in the first place because they believe in an omnipotent God.

The law of acceleration, as noted by Albert Einstein, $E=mc2$, is the relationship between mass and energy. It is the equation of what it takes to generate the energy of change, (victim, cross to bear crossover). Similarly, Newton's law of motion $F=ma$ equation: for a mass to move, a force must be applied and for energy to be released, force must accelerate, (the loud clarion call of a soul that won't let you rest.) In a spiritual awakening, the force applied is unrest. Increasing the level of force moves the mass faster and releases the amount of energy it takes to bring the soul into purview and alignment. In a state of true consciousness, we will know the law of creation is a universal law. In harmony with the Universe, the more of us co-creating with the Universe to manifest what is in the highest good of all unleashes the magic and possibility of experiencing heaven on earth.

When you are co-creating you will observe that certain key indicators are present; your perception has shifted from one of fear (ego-driven) to one of love (the realm of God). Another is you will feel compelled to act. You want to herald the Good News of possibilities, sometimes in a loud and boisterous way, but also in the silent way of the water that can be observed as it shapes the rocks of the riverbed. Through your new love language, you will understand the signs, and signals of the Universe and can begin to feel synchronicities occurring all around you. The call you were about to make when the phone rings and the call is from the person you were about to call.

Another clue you are aware of co-creating with the Universe is when you have fully surrendered. You have to let go and let God. You categorically know you have done your part to secure what you have named, so all you have to do now is step out of the way and let the Universe deliver the other half of the equation as promised because it is already done. Ask and thou shall be given.

The second stage of creation, rest, is the state that allows the Universe time to put into action what you have claimed. It delivers by bringing into your life people or things to help facilitate the delivery of that which you have claimed into your universe. Think of it as a barren land finally getting rainfall. All the dormant seeds were waiting for was the right conditions to manifest. As you interact with the resources delivered to you, it's now your turn to choose how to put your creation into action and decide which of them best facilitates the vision you claimed.

Let me use my own story here. My mantra throughout my adult life was I just needed to be free. I further defined "free to be myself" as my choices being separate from all outside influences. I began writing a list of all the things I liked and didn't like about me that kept me feeling in bondage. What I found was the things I liked about myself were also the things I didn't like about myself; I am responsible, I am resilient, I am unique, and I can fix it. These were the very same qualities keeping me in bondage and away from who I wanted to become. I therefore decided I wanted to express the "fruits of the spirit" (love, joy, peace, patience, kindness, goodness, faithfulness, gentleness, which I called self-control). Why that was important to me was because I felt if I were those things all the time, I would be free. The qualities I possessed were great and I wanted to use them to create the life I wanted, not the life expected of me. I wanted to build a business that was my own. I wanted to dance. I wanted to dress as if I were a walking piece of art instead of in constricting business suits. I wanted to surround myself with beauty and I wanted to be seen as brand new. I truly wanted to just be Kiana; the Kiana I knew whom no one else did. The thing is you can only hear yourself when you are still. Being at rest allows you to identify and recognize the resources needed to water your garden. Rest is the precursor to putting things in motion.

All the experiences good and bad and the changes I needed to make brought me to where I am today. Now, every time I want to claim something for my life, these are the steps I walk through in Faith, Hope, and Love.

The Unfolding Stages of Creation.

The moment you name and claim what you desire is the moment the wheels of creation start to turn. When you name things it is very powerful and every time you speak the name, you are sending the vibrational frequency into the world and it bounces back to you as yes because the universe only knows how to say yes. For example, let's take a limiting belief. If you believe you are not enough the universe says yes. If you believe you are good enough the universe says yes, so it is imperative you name and claim your true desires. We claim and name things over ourselves all the time and what we name is what we'll get. Naming it is the first part of creation and then you begin seeding the why it's important to you. When you are setting out to create a business, or a relationship, think about what you want the experience to be. Visualize that experience; what it looks like, what it makes you feel, what behaviors are needed from yourself, and what actions are necessary from you and others to accomplish the vision. Finally claim it, believe it, and what you believe you can achieve. You will now have a guided map for yourself and for becoming a guide to a soul in search of itself. And that soul will hear you without uttering a word. Inspired actions can change the lives of so many in need, and because you know the language of the universe and that it has your back, it can be empowering, joyous, and effortless to help others on their way to an awakening.

Naming it.

Naming what you want with clarity and certainty is tantamount to an art form. I had to learn how to name what it was I truly wanted for my life by going through the process of shedding the burdens keeping me bound to the ego world. All the steps I went through from therapy to plant-based support were all a part of the process to get to a point where I could unequivocally name what I wanted for my life. Naming "it" led right into my "Yes" and then into the action to manifest what I envisioned.

What is that thing you want to manifest in your lifetime? What is it that you want to sculpt and create with your new eyes? Whether claiming is subconscious or conscious because of being universally connected, the soul understands. And what you claim is what the universe brings into form. It's important that this is understood because the things claimed are who we will become, so it is crucial to be crystal clear about your heart and spirit's desires. Carefully and thoughtfully embrace things to be manifested. It is only then that it must be named because the law of cause and effect is now fully engaged. It leads to a new house always imbued with faith hope and love, the superpowers of spirit.

Claiming I AM.

I AM was given to Moses as the name of God we can speak. I AM is powerful. I mean it only has three letters and a space. Using I AM is claiming for yourself that as a being of God, I AM. Everything that comes after it is a declaration of what is to come. "You shall not take the name of the Lord your God in vain for the Lord will not hold him guiltless who takes His name in vain." Exodus 20:7. I AM is a common response. When this teaching became clear to me, I began tracking how many times I used "I AM" casually. It was daunting the number of times I said I AM. Add to that I usually ended with something I did not want to declare over myself. As I fully understand the power of I AM, I now focus on saying this powerful phrase and say I AM when I am claiming something of importance over my life.

Acknowledgment and Awareness are what bring you face-to-face with this notion of I AM and I was surprised by my results.

An Awareness Exercise: begin by tracking how many times you say I AM in a day, in an hour, in a conversation with someone you are close to. The first time I did this I got to ten in twenty minutes or so. It was daunting how many times I was using the Lord's name in vain.

Instead of saying I AM shift to I FEEL:

I AM........ hungry   to   I feel hungry
I AM........ tired   to   I feel tired
I AM........ overwhelmed   to   I feel overwhelmed

This shift will create an amazing lift in your energy. Remember if you do want to claim something over your life, being intentional about it is very important.

Acceptance follows Awareness. Once you accept your limiting belief influences your actions, you can begin to create the life you imagine.

Practice for I AM: Faith, Hope, Love, and the greatest of these is love…in action

The four A's of I AM: **Acknowledgement, Awareness, Acceptance, and Action.**

Acknowledgment: The act of recognizing or admitting the existence of the truth of something. Also expressing gratitude for the discovery.

Awareness: refers to the state or quality of being conscious, cognizant, or mindful of something or recognition of one's surroundings, thoughts, feelings, or experiences. Awareness can also refer to being alert, attentive, or observant of external stimuli or internal processes. It encompasses the ability to perceive, comprehend, and be sensitive to oneself, others, and the environment. It can range from a basic level of consciousness to a deeper level of self-awareness or mindfulness.

Acceptance: The act of agreeing to or approving something. It involves embracing recognition—its validity

Action: A behavior or movement that is performed in response to a stimulus or intention. It involves carrying out a specific task or activity, often with a purpose or goal in mind. It also refers to the process of taking steps to achieve a desired outcome or result.

Here Are Some Of My Practices.

First, I was brought into awareness a truth previously unknown to me. I became aware of the signals my body was giving me. For example, I always I often tense up or feel irritated whenever someone was around or spoke to me. The sensations in my body were key indicators of how I felt. I would then ask myself, *What is it about this person/experience that upsets me? What does this tell me about myself?* I soon learned my triggers disconnected me from feeling love within myself and were signals that everything bothering me was something for me to let go of.

Next, I acknowledged the truth of the situation and began to track whatever the feelings were. I began to ask, *Why do I feel this way? What am I making this mean about myself?* This is where the limiting belief comes in. It took me a while before I could connect my limiting beliefs to my emotional state. Many times, I would hear my beliefs in my conversations. Someone would say, "Let me help you," and I would say, "I don't need help or that's ok, I don't want to bother you." And there it was, and man does it show where you are stuck! I don't need help is a sign. I don't want to bother you underlies the sign. Who but you said you are a bother? When you begin to recognize in yourself or others what limiting beliefs are, it unlocks a gateway into your healing. We state our truth all the time, so begin listening for it. Document it and you'll begin to see that you do know what your limiting beliefs are. Once I was brought to a new level of awareness of the root cause of the limiting beliefs triggering me, I acknowledged and thanked it for uncovering itself to me. For me, this part is important because it unknowingly brings love and compassion to how I respond to things.

If you are unaware of how limiting beliefs keep you from loving yourself and others, it's not your fault. It is nothing to feel shame or guilt about. They are automatic responses to your conditioning that need to be unlearned. These experiences allow you to sit with what you see and assess how you feel about the ways they have kept you from yourself. Now unconditionally love yourself around your limitations. Yes, it is so. Yes, I do that. Ok got it. That is acceptance. Unconditional love has no conditions, judgments, or expectations. It just is. Relief comes in letting go of control. Now I am surrendered and can see, feel, know, and understand that I AM that I AM. I completed the first step in acknowledging and facing my pain. To know where I was headed I had to know from where I was coming.

The I AM in Action.

Practice And Do It Every Day. The More You Do It, The More It Becomes You.

Using the tenets of the Emissary Wheel there were exercises based on Faith, Hope, and Love that got me closer to the I AM. The big takeaway was my understanding of the story and the five concepts that mirrored the stages of my spiritual growth: Here are some examples of my stories I had to overcome. I started creating stories like the one below to help me along the way. My stories were as follows.

> STORY: I know I am wise. My sister-in-law repeatedly tells me so. But I have this belief system that wise people sit on a mountain of their truth and I never wanted that for myself as I always wanted to be relatable. So often, whether at home, in business, or in social situations I don't allow my wisdom to shine.

> FAITH: I held myself back from showing people how wise I am, which kept me away from people who I really wanted to be with.

> HOPE: That made me feel lonely.

> LOVE: I fully accept I created everything I see and feel. I fully love and respect myself.

> I AM Wise. I create within myself a sense of wonder from the wisdom I embody from Source. I feel love and joy and being myself. I am free to share the wisdom within. I AM Wise

> STORY: In writing this book and sharing my truth with the world I was afraid of what people would think about my family and was truly uncertain it would not cause an irreparable rift. But denying the existence of those truths was absolutely counter to the work I was doing and the gaping

holes demanded the full truth, the yummy parts, and the parts I was inclined to hide.

FAITH: I see how my fear of hurting others, especially my family, limited my ability to heal and share my story. Positively walking through Faith, Hope, and Love made me certain I was going to share the story.

HOPE: As a result of not being certain I felt if I did share the story I would lose my family.

LOVE: I fully accept I created everything I see and feel. I fully love and respect myself. I am certain and courageous. Positively walking through Faith, Hope, and Love put me in the certainty that I was going to share the story and do so with love. Now I feel with certainty it's a gateway to everyone's healing, and my love and courage free me from my fear. I AM Certain and Courageous.

Even with compassion high on my list of virtues, I learned an important lesson about compassion from my daughter.

STORY: My middle child always tells me she doesn't feel good so she can't go to school. Later, I realized she was manipulating me and angrily told her from here on out she didn't have the luxury of being sick. One day she got sick and I didn't let her stay home because I didn't believe her. The fact is she was sick and had to be sent home from school.

FAITH: Through this incident, I saw I didn't have compassion for my daughter for how she truly felt, and in the compassion department I still had work to do.

HOPE: It made me feel crappy.

LOVE: **I** fully accept I created everything I see and feel. I fully love and respect myself. I Am Compassion. I create compassion and curiosity whenever someone says I don't feel well. This helps me feel connected to them and myself. Together we come to a way to move forward, stay home, or go to school. I AM compassion.

STORY: I could love beyond conditions. Three years ago, I was dating someone who had unresolved trauma in his life. On a trip to San Diego, he unleashed some of his anger on me due to the frustrations he was experiencing. Being able to see beyond his pain I felt a great deal of compassion for him and though I no longer wanted to date him, I wanted to show him compassion.

FAITH: That I could see when someone else gets activated and especially if that triggered me, I could go to the source of what's keeping me disconnected and feel tremendous love and gratitude for someone who needed my compassion.

HOPE: Love and profound gratitude that I was capable of unconditional love

LOVE: I fully accept I created everything I see and feel I fully love and respect myself. I Am Compassion.

STORY: On my journey patience was one of the areas I felt more competent in. It showed up in the workplace as well as in my personal life. People who worked for me who were promoted or new to the organization would often face the impatience of others for not grasping their responsibilities right away. My employees would look to me because I was aware change is a part of the process and that learning is a discovery. I could listen to them with compassion, grace, and patience and allow for what they needed to succeed in our organization. In my personal life, I have three amazing children, all different, who have shown me my patience. As with all teenagers who need to separate for their psychological well-being behaviors such as their talking back, not doing their chores, breaking the rules being upset, their defiance are all challenges I am walking through and appreciating my gift of patience.

FAITH: I have a lot of patience for people to grow, expand, and make mistakes and I belief this will lead to learning the skills that are valuable to our organization.

HOPE: For me, I get a sense of joy in the accomplishment of others and I feel so good about their achievements, and in turn, I feel appreciation for my ability to be patient and I feel so much peace.

LOVE: I fully accept I created everything I see and feel and I fully love and respect myself. I AM Patience.

STORY: Holding on to my family, money, and comfort was all an illusion of control and shallow in the realm of my spiritual journey. I truly thought I was going to lose something, family, myself, and my sanity but here I am on the other side and I have lost nothing. None of those things were true.

FAITH: Without seeing the full picture, I was holding on so tight I was limiting myself to the possibilities and so I stayed where I was. On the other side when I saw the depth of my need to control the status quo and that there was nothing to lose I found everything. And the deeper I go into this work the more and more I understand how the illusions of this world are made true.

HOPE: When I felt I was losing something, I felt desperate. When I realized I had nothing to lose it was bliss.

LOVE: I fully accept I created everything I see and feel I fully love and respect myself. I Am Generous.

STORY: When I was at McDonalds early on in my tenure we had a season when sales were very low and we were worried about meeting payroll. On the day of payroll, we had no money in the bank to meet it. People in management were frantic but for some reason, I wasn't because I believed in the abundance and prosperity of the universe. Just before payroll was due like magic a large, unexpected deposit was made to our account, and the day after, the same was repeated. I AM Abundance and prosperity.

FAITH: What you claim over your life is true…even when in fear claim abundance. I got in tune with all the positive things I wanted to claim in my life…and even the negative things.

HOPE: It alleviated the stress of running the business.

LOVE: I fully accept I created everything I see and feel I fully love and respect myself. I Am Abundance.

STORY: It took a lot of courage to do all I did as a child and into adulthood. This courage to fill in and take on responsibilities for my family came from the divinity within me. I never thought I couldn't do it. I just did it because it needed to be done and I was given the capacity to do it.

The place where I lacked courage was in having tough, honest conversations with my family about my fears and depression because it would show my weakness of not being enough. All of these were my limiting beliefs but they existed in my reality and held me back from getting what I needed. It was the work of discovering myself that took profound courage to see what I didn't want to see and feel what I didn't want to feel and move forward anyway.

Faith seeing who I have become:

FAITH Courageous behaviors: I became responsible and resilient courageously filling in the gaps for my family; courageously speaking to power in meetings and sharing my thoughts to bring us together

HOPE: Feeling the lessening of pressure and freedom having the tough conversations with my family

LOVE: Now that I see. I fully accept I created everything I see and I fully love and respect myself. I Am courage

STORY: I did not love basketball. When I was in high school I experienced a joy not from basketball but from the people on the team who just gelled and together we achieved so much. The team spirit was my driver...when it was time to go to college and my parents wanted me to get a basketball scholarship I chose a school with the same ethos of my high school. Unfortunately, the experience was so different and the team lacked the cohesion that drove me, so I stopped playing sports altogether and to this day avoid basketball. Even now when my son asks me to play basketball with him I find every reason not to.

FAITH: My experience in college created a world where I disconnected from team sports and did not have the opportunity to experience another great sports team. I created a narrative that basketball was painful and this stopped me from playing with my son.

HOPE: I felt guilty and sad that the story I created prevented me from enjoying what could have been great bonding with my son and I felt badly that he had to experience sadness around my story.

LOVE: I fully accept I created everything I see and feel I fully love and respect myself. I Am Joy.

Every time I see a new truth about myself, I follow my I AM statements with a new creation over myself. I begin with my I AM statement, followed by what I want to see and feel and how I want to love. Then with the same I AM statement, I claim it once again and live into it. I use the principles of the Emissary Wheel to navigate the shift I am creating. Not everyone will see the shift within me right away as it takes time for others and me to fully embody the shift. as I move into a new way of being to stay on my path of self-love. Grace and all the principles of the wheel are available for me to embrace.

Thinking Differently

Two Trees…I AM

The concept of the two trees may be mind-bending but I want to introduce this concept to readers well on their way on a spiritual journey. It is part of understanding the I AM.

In Genesis, the first book of the Bible is about creation, and we are taught *The Tree of Life* represents everlasting Life, infinity, and eternity, while the *Tree of Knowledge of Good and Evil* leads to a path of destruction, and surely physical death. Who would choose death? Something about this picture didn't sit well with me.

When I was a child, as I noted earlier, I was always looking for the *little light of mine,* so that *I could let it shine.* Unable to find it, I had numerous questions about my faith birthed in Christianity. I questioned everything. The messages encoded in gospel music, the story of Mary Magdalene, and top of mind, questions about the story of the two trees. My burning question, which never seemed to have an answer was so what's between the two trees? I never understood why anyone would think one tree should be more important than the other tree. If the *Tree of Knowledge of Good and Evil* is by conventional worldview, a path that eventually leads to disaster and destruction, and *The Tree of Life* to salvation, then why would anyone choose destruction, and why would God put both trees in the garden if they both weren't necessary? Why would a God who makes no mistakes, create these two trees? In my opinion, each tree has a purpose and is equally important. Both trees represent choice—free will. Together they represent the full potential of our world.

Newborns seemingly come into the world knowing nothing. The fact is, they are not *tabula rasa (*clean slate*); instead, they are a glass* that is filled with air, not empty at all. Imprints of the physical universe already exist in this baby, parents' DNA, for one.

Consider the fact that at birth babies may be in between the two trees but closer to the *Tree of Life* because their souls are not yet buried under morass and emotional baggage and are therefore closer to Source and more accepting of all possibilities. As human experiences enter their lives, that which is dominated by the fruits from the *Tree of Good and Evil* choice becomes a part of their existence and they move closer to that tree. Were they to be at the midpoint between each tree, they might have an appreciation of the benefits of both trees. What the *Tree of Knowledge of Good and Evil* offers is the duality of existence. Generally, duality is necessary to comprehend choice. Since a benevolent God would not make anything without a purpose, the *Tree of Good and Evil* most definitely has a purpose. Like everything else on earth, these two trees represent duality; the opposite ends of a spectrum: life and death.

To kick the can further down the road, let's ask the question; what happens if one stays midway between the two trees? Is it possible then, to have a front-row seat to all that happens in both worlds, and therefore be able to make the best choice for life and enjoy both worlds equally? Would one want to live without knowledge, just accepting that everlasting life is preferable to knowledge? So, I ask again, what is between the two trees? What separated them? If one were to draw a line between both trees and walk the path what would be the experience? Like the dashes on your headstone 1927—2024 representing birth and death in the physical realm, I believe the dashes between the trees represent choice. One experiences a journey based on the tree of choice Equilibrium is to remain midpoint between both trees. The trees themselves are simply vessels holding free will.

Landing squarely on the path of the *Tree of Knowledge and Good and Evil* means full indulgence in all the world has to offer, good and bad. If you feed only from the *Tree of Life* does that mean you remain ignorant to choice? What then would be the value of the trees? I now see that I AM both trees. The tree of eternal life is my soul, that which never dies and the tree of knowledge of good and evil is my body and what lies between and throughout is Spirit. It's all connected and living as one. I AM a powerful creator as we all are. What we create stems from the way we see ourselves. If we see our human selves first then maybe spirit and divinity/ soul we will always be seeking truth from a place where we will never find satisfaction, success, peace, or the surprise and wonder in being ourselves. When we follow the order of creation, soul first, then spirit, then human, we will experience life from a place of freedom and love. This is especially true as you are learning to love yourself unconditionally.

The interconnectedness of everything is the I AM: Reconnecting to Source returns you to the I AM

At birth, babies are connected to their mothers by an umbilical cord and their fontanelle (some believe full connection to Source) does not fuse until eighteen months of age. Wide open, babies remain close to Source. If you have children, I am sure you have marveled at their innocence and openness. They completely trust their caregiver, they cry when hungry, poop when they need, and until about three or four they have no filters;

they often have imaginary friends (maybe not imagined): they talk to trees as though they are talking to anyone and anything else, and they view everything without judgment. Incidentally, if you put a human fingerprint next to the marking of a tree stump they are indistinguishable at a macro level. Imagine how empowering it could be if we were able to retain these qualities into adulthood while adding value insights garnered from the world we live in. What an empowering feeling of true freedom when Source seamlessly integrates with our worldly lives. Could we not appreciate that we are the creators of our lives? Our Destiny?

Understanding that you are God and God is you is profound. In this dominion, you will finally come to understand you are more than your thoughts and feelings, and in fact, are an infinite being with limitless potential. You are the I AM. I've come to believe and know I AM the I AM. The moment you change your perception of the "world" and recognize this phenomenon, is the moment you will begin accruing the benefits of the total Universe where everything is one with God's infinite wisdom. Man and nature are in perfect harmony and represent our higher, Godly selves.

I AM Affirmations

- I choose to live at my highest potential every day.
- I live fully present to the divine purpose of my human life.
- I Am invincible and connected to the light. I Am Divine and I AM Positive!
- I AM the peace, power, and presence of Divinity. I carry the spirit of God wherever I go and God carries me also
- I fully embrace and love all of myself leaving no part of me separate from the unconditional love that surrounds me and is within me at all times.
- I lovingly release the past and turn my attention to this generous present moment. All is well

- I AM worthy and love myself unconditionally
- I rest within the great womb Mother, I am one with all, connected to every part of life and existence
- I AM love joy peace patience kindness goodness faithfulness gentleness and self-control
- I receive love understanding and caring from others, and acknowledge it with gratitude; I am seen, heard, and held at all times, experiencing the greatest love from all that is and created for my good
- Every energy center in my body is open, bringing my unique essence to the world, I set it free to do what it is meant to do, with love, joy, peace, patience, kindness, goodness, faithfulness, gentleness, and self-control from the highest power for the highest good of all
- Everything I am engaging in, prospers
- I attract others with good intentions, as we all flourish
- I invite love, intimacy, vulnerability, pleasure, fun, laughter, and commitment into my life
- I AM a walking prayer, giving and receiving the magic of life- I live at the highest vibration
- I feel invincible and connected to the light. I am divine and I am positive
- I lovingly create my own reality. I am open and receptive to blessings. God and me, me, and God are one
- The universe loves and supports me. I release the past and reclaim my good now. God and me, me, and God are one
- Natural order establishes the process for my good. Trust HER I Am
- I AM the embodiment of divine love, co-creating my perfect world
- I AM a beacon of joy, compassion, peace, and love, surrendering to the healing within

- I AM the embodiment of divine love and sensuality, manifesting my perfect world through stillness and sacred action
- I AM supported by the universe and my celestial guides, constantly aligning with my highest truth and divine purpose
- I AM the creator of my perfect world, rooted in courage and wrapped in the embrace of divine connection
- I AM a beacon of joy, clarity, and agape love, reflecting my inner truth and boundless potential
- I AM the embodiment of love and grace in the pursuit of excellence
- I AM a beacon of spiritual growth and personal transformation
- I AM the architect of my spiritual landscape, crafting each moment with intention and grace
- I AM a beacon of connectivity, shining light on the unity that binds us all in spiritual kinship

Affirmation Prayer

God. I receive it. Holy one I receive it. I receive love, joy peace, patience kindness, goodness, faithfulness, and self-control. Whatever plans you have for me I receive it. Thank you. I receive it.

I take back my vitality and energy and feel more and more healthy each and every day. My body knows how to heal. My body knows how to heal!

Natural order establishes the process for my good. I Trust HER. I AM.

CHAPTER TWELVE
THINGS I LEARNED ALONG THE WAY

☥

Humility

I don't know. When asked a question that I didn't have an answer to or any knowledge of, being able to admit out loud that I didn't know released the pressure of always needing to be on. I am not arrogant enough to think that only I have answers. This has always been my strength as a collaborator to seek advice from those who might have the answers I seek. As a CEO I wanted and still want, to find ways for everyone to shine their inner light. The more the merrier because what we create together can be ever-expanding, and long-lasting. It is said that humility is a virtue, an unpretentious way of looking at oneself. I hope this to be true for all of us, however, I know that I will remain humble and grateful in this life.

Spiritual Growth

Do you remember as a child standing against the wall and getting a mark for each year of your growth? Growing to spiritual maturation has measured yardsticks too. The emergence of the authentic self in a world set to the clock of normal will show changes. Your circle will change. You may lose friends. You might even find yourself alone. Relationships may be few but they are meaningful and sustaining. Nature will be observed with new eyes as the miracle it is, and you will know the sacred geometry of all things. Sacred geometry is the natural forms, numbers, and patterns we see repeatedly that make up the natural world—how a Lady Slipper orchid looks like a ballerina or the shape of a cloud looks like a teapot. It's a fascinating subject and worth investigating what each of the symbols, patterns, and numbers mean. For example, circles in sacred geometry can be thought of as a symbol of oneness and duality. If you cut a circle, at each end of the now straight line its its opposite, let's say love and hate. Now rejoin the circle, love, and hate are the same and suggest completeness. In other words, if one can love one can also hate, but with no judgment, it is just what it is—an emotion.

What will grow in leaps and bounds is your unshakable self-identity. You will arrive at a place where you know your infinite source. Approaching your full spiritual growth, at the top of your vertical growth spurt, you will have a deep connection with Source and a feeling of true well-being. Your sense of purpose will be crystal clear and your need to share the goodness you have found with others, compelling.

Spiritual Responsibility

Spiritual Responsibility is choice and belief. Words like self-discipline, courage, and integrity will be parts of your spiritual vocabulary. Embracing Connection, Compassion, and Communion will be natural. Making the right choices for you will become a standard solely yours. But with every choice you make accepting responsibility and being accountable for that choice opens the possibility of freedom from story and hurt.

Connection

Think of a telephone line connected under sea through landlines, or in the air through cell towers. That connectivity links us to our loved ones, business associates, and even strangers. If there is one thing that sets the soul on fire, it is meaningful connections. I am sure you've walked into a room and your intuition antennae begin a mad buzz when around some people. If the buzz feels negative, this may be because your connecting frequencies are not on the same wavelength. If it's positive you'll feel drawn to that person. When positive energies come together as one it radiates far and wide and is infectious. Modern science has proven that there is an electromagnetic field around us and our hearts. Many scientists believe it to be the infinite and overlapping connection of humanity.

There is nothing more empowering than connections. Connections can provide a safety net of trust, love, and support. To know there are people in your tribe you can count on gives the kind of peace that is ineffable. Meaningful connections are active. Shared interest, total honesty, mindful behaviors, and meaningful conversations are all part of building connections that last. The benefits of creating a life of positivity support not only social well-being but promote mental, physical, spiritual, and emotional well-being as well. The most significant connection is the one you have with yourself and the divine.

Compassion

Compassion is simply kindness. Though it is related to sympathy (pity) and empathy (understanding), compassion involves active listening and a true understanding of you and your unique needs. Self-less compassionate people then do something to improve the situation.

Communion

Is a time to remember the sacrifices that have been made on our behalf. It is also a time to remember that we are all connected and that making room for each other and helping to carry the burden of each other makes us resist the ego and fall more in line with the Divine Plan.

Focus

As a CEO, the myriad things thrown at me were endless. I had to learn to master time and that meant mastering focus. Miraculously I was able to complete all my responsibilities without sacrificing quality because the one thing I had mastered was how to effectively work with people to live out the acronym TEAM. I trusted my employees, I delegated and I saw them as equally important to accomplishing our goals as myself, which was not a stretch as many were ready to bring their best selves to the table. We all were involved in creating the life we wanted as individuals and to do so we needed a collective approach to achieving our results while maintaining our unique way of fulfilling our assignments. We each had a role to play in our success. Our ability to focus was increased by the fact that we each did it in a way that worked best for us.

Outer focus leads to excellence in our "normal" world while inner focus leads to excellence in the quality of our inner lives. A Glorious Arising assumes a life in outer focus is ready to shift gears and its attention to inner focus. Inner focus requires developing the practices that get you in touch with who you truly are in total awareness of the present moment. Practicing mindfulness through tools like meditation, yoga, journaling, breathwork, prayer, honing your instincts, fasting, acquainting yourself with your compassion meter, practicing unconditional love, faith, and hope, and getting in touch with your God self is enormously helpful. The confidence you gain from spiritual focus, i.e., forging a connection with source, returns infinite gifts.

Integrity

We are all well aware of integrity in the human plane. People have it or they don't. The book is focused on the spiritual aspects of integrity. Integrity here is discernment. Spiritual integrity unveils the control of the mind often masked as our protector and encourages deep self-analysis. According to Jac O'Keeffe, in his blog on *Spiritual Integrity*, demands "brutal self-honesty, considerable depth of self-awareness and an uncompromising willingness to be authentic." He further goes on to say, "Spiritual integrity requires us to unconditionally love and respect ourselves."

Integrity indeed allows us to grow into our God self and to mature in our spiritual practice. In oneness, where love exists, we can embrace humanity while remaining, humble, honest, vulnerable, and reliable.

Giving is Receiving

I'm often asked why I give my love away so readily. The simple truth is I give that love to myself at the same time that I'm extending love to others. In giving, I'm receiving. People will usually follow up with, "Well, what you gave to that person was not reciprocated. You got nothing back so what are you receiving?"

The way I see it is, if I give my love unconditionally to someone who is not ready to receive it, I receive the benefit of my unconditional love. If I withhold my unconditional love from someone then what I receive is the withholding of my unconditional love.

Often we're looking for an equal response from someone, and that's conditioned love—I'll give to you if you give to me first. Conditional love doesn't feel good to me at all. Unconditional is just that. It's that internal peace, joy, and love that comes from the experience of giving that matters to me. Unconditional love does not seek a response. It is just what it is. That is the joy of giving. I have worked hard not to block the blessing of someone giving or pouring into my life because I understand that if I do, I am blocking their blessing of loving themselves as well as the experience of me receiving love from someone else's giving. Giving and receiving are instantaneous if your love is unconditional.

Here and Now. Being Present.

Have you tried to sit for five minutes doing nothing? No email. No text, no social media, no TV...absolutely no distraction. It's hard right?

Maybe for some, unbearable. Engaging in activity after activity to avoid the present moment, is often a sign of fear—fear of looking inward. If you are living in the past or the future you will miss all that is happening in the now. And truly, isn't a life lived moment-to-moment? Every moment is all you have and as the saying goes, 'In the blink of an eye life can change.' From my journey, I now understand that the past, present, and future are not linear but co-exist. In the spiritual world you'll come to learn there is no past, present, or future but let's leave that for book two. Just suffice it to say current scientific theories of space and time suggest the past, present, and future are all equally real–and fundamentally indistinguishable, and therefore in 'reality' the past and the future are happening now.

Being present includes awareness and the power of observation. One of the great visionaries of our time, Steve Jobs, proffered mindfulness as the way to pursue self-interest and self-enlightenment which he argues only betters our society. (Inc Magazine article). "It is in mindfulness," Jobs states, "there is room to hear the more subtle things the universe is trying to engage."

Change (Spiritual Transformation)

Change is a humdinger. It comes with the gnashing of teeth and much kicking and screaming. It is one of the hardest things to achieve and it's scary. It is hard to change because our disconnected human psychology tricks us into believing it's safe to stay put rather than step into the uncertain. Repeated behaviors of any kind create grooves in our brains called habits. Habits put impulse behaviors on automatic pilot, but once you have attained a level of spiritual maturity, change will effortlessly become a part of who you are. Why? Because a fundamental change to your spirit devoid of fear or uncertainty has occurred. Yet change happens in our lives all the time…a sudden illness, the loss of a family member, or the end of a love are all changes we experience and somehow carry on.

Setting out on a spiritual path engages change. Change questions our notion of a static identity, and change is what fills the gap between who you are and who you want to be. This gap is called transformation. Embracing change helps mitigate the tides that come during a transformation. Yet it is through change that we can come face-to-face with our true potential. Through the tools and activities, mentioned earlier, such as meditation, prayer, observing nature, and quiet time, the uncertainty of the 'past' will be stripped away allowing you to walk into your new life with spiritual elegance.

Patience

I don't have the ability to change how someone else thinks, believes, or feels, ever. The only thing that I can change is how I think, feel, and believe about myself, others, and about all of life. There are moments when I find myself feeling anxious or antsy and then I remember, *oh* this is a teachable moment. In time, with patience, I will usually learn what lesson it is that I was to learn.

Living in LA, I often find myself in traffic. I've learned that no matter how anxious or frustrated I become, it doesn't change the fact that I'm stuck in traffic. What I learned is that things were the way they were for a reason always. It's teaching me about myself and there was no need to be anxious or frustrated about traffic that I knew I was going to sit in. That in turn gave me an access point to my patience. In life there were so many things that I wanted to go a certain way and bound by time and expectation of when I was going to accomplish something. While deadlines are important, I'm very clear that my ability to feel and experience patience eases the way and creates within me peace.

Inspiration

In January of 2023, for my forty-fifth birthday, one of my best friends, Tammy, and I traveled to Bali to spend our birthdays together. My sister-in-law, Amy helped set up the trip for us. I desired to create a cultural, spiritual, and restful trip. While there, we had the blessing of touring around the country with our guide, Dewa, who took such good care of us. One day he took us sightseeing. We stopped at a local artisan shop where men and women were carving wood into the shapes of nature, mostly in personifications of the deities of their Hindu traditions. These artisans had many different jobs and only came together to create a masterpiece when they were inspired. They didn't force it or deny it. They allowed inspiration to come and with peace and joy let what they saw unfold.

Another of our stops was to spend time with the family of a man who was a prominent member of his village. His mission was to teach youngsters and visitors to his country Balinese traditions. He lovingly took us into his home and there we ate and learned about honoring the land, the food, and especially ourselves. Here I saw how everything they needed was grown by them. Life was so simple. Everyone we met on this trip was lovely. I, without knowing it at the time was being inspired to reconnect to the land. You see, I have always been connected to Earth. I walk barefoot in the grass, need the sun on my face, and because I live in California spend most of my days outside.

Like in a Balinese home, my bedroom is open-air and has no walls other than structural. Even so, when I came home from Bali I could no longer sleep through the night which for me was completely out of the ordinary. Though the nights were colder, I was inspired to and began sleeping outside on a daybed positioned near my bedroom. Because of Bali, I was inspired to deepen my connection to nature and Mother Earth, realizing I too was nature—and in harmony, I was an integral part of the whole of this earthly existence I embody. That trip further helped me to understand how connected *all* of us are. For a person who intensely dislikes camping, I have now set up a permanent outdoor living experience. Who knew? I just simply answered the call of inspiration.

Inspiration itself is transcendent. Inspired people have changed the world with a single thought put into action. Think of Steve Jobs. His vision inspired the creation of Apple, and good or bad, changed the lives of countless people. But what exactly is inspiration? It is access to our higher self that guides desires, dreams, and goals into a state of bliss. It may come in the form of creativity, motivation; and other positive attributes and is most likely to be present when all systems are in harmony.

I find inspiration all around me. When someone talks to me now, instead of cringing as in my past, I often find myself listening and thinking, Oh, that's a business idea. In my mind, I have already created all kinds of ways it will grow and help people. Every day I receive hundreds of ideas and most pass in the moment forgotten as the next activity or thought takes its place. There are some though that I feel inspired to write down. I know if not now, someday they may come in handy, if not for me, then for someone else. I have learned that all the ideas I have are mostly not for me to launch. It is the creative force within people that inspires me the most.

You never know when inspiration will hit. When it does I pray you do not ignore it. That you see the promise of what inspires you unfold into the miraculous result you desire.

The Power of Prayer

One of the most important spiritual exercises, is prayer. A direct communication channel to Source, prayer is not just a pathway to awakening but also acts as a shield against the demands of the outer world. If you believe in the power of prayer and fully surrender your heart in earnest, all the earth and everything in it will respond to you. You may have heard people say miracles happen through prayer. For me, this is true because here I am standing in God's favor. The private time between you and Source allows you to build successful relations both in the physical and spiritual worlds. I used to imagine praying into a cup before giving it to someone I loved. Now I pray into my glass of water. Water holds memory and as water is consumed it travels to every cell in our bodies so insert your prayer into water. The transformation is incredible.

Remember it is your belief that inspires your prayers, manifestations, and requests.

Music

A per Stevie Wonder, living "In the Key of Life," is pure pleasure. It is a unifying force of the universe. Every culture, every person, much like they have language, has music that makes a connection beyond self. From time immemorial, music has been at the center of spiritual life. The divine power of music somehow has the ability to connect with the wavelength and frequency of our souls and can transport us to a realm greater than ourselves. Physiologically, it lights up our limbic system and floods us with dopamine, our happy hormone. Whether we create, listen to, or play music, it has the same calming and transcendental qualities to enhance our spiritual growth.

Dance

This is another miracle tool that strengthens the immune system and promotes healing by reducing stress and tension. Dance focuses attention and brings about a change in consciousness and physical fitness. Dance and music are well-known practices used in health and wellness to reduce stress, prevent disease, and manage moods. Dance-like music impacts the level of the feel-good hormones, this time serotonin, in promoting a sense of joy. No wonder my soul knew it wanted to dance way before I knew about a spiritual journey.

Community Involvement

 As I have discussed throughout this book, we are all part of a universal consciousness and our journey back to the soul is an effort to reconnect to the whole. As siloed humans, we are cut off from the energy of the collective and feel a sense of aloneness. As the bible says when two or more are gathered in his name there I AM. Not everyone around you will be on an ascension journey, but their love and support as you go through it is a gift. My gifts were the women and men who supported me on my journey. Amy, Anthony, Tammy, Akil, and Mercedes along with my team helped me build the foundational pieces of Glorious Arisings. Thomas, Dalia, and Jenny, all of whom witnessed growth and we were and still are on the journey together.

As we named it, Agape love is the zenith of a spiritual life. Communities represent the connection of an individual to the collective. Communities therefore provide the kinds of support, relationships, and encouragement that make our everyday lives easier and Agape love profound.

Journaling

Allows us to process our emotions in a safe and private space. It tracks patterns, holds us accountable, allows moment-by-moment self-awareness, allows goal setting, and is very therapeutic and cathartic. It doubles down as a form of anxiety and stress reliever as it records the history of our progress. Spiritual journaling documents the path to our awakening. In the physical state, journaling helps to boost memory, comprehension, and overall cognitive processing.

Immersive walks with nature

I love nature. I love the feel of the grass under my feet and the sun on my face. Can you imagine a life without nature? It is impossible. Our entire world's economy, society, and survival depend on nature, its ecosystem services our every need. Our basic happiness, health, and prosperity depend on nature and we have taken it for granted. The rivers and oceans, streams and sea, the soil producing the fruits and vegetables we eat; the air we breathe, and our circle of life partners provide additional foods. The chicken, the cow, the lamb, the bees, and birds, are all in the dance of life with us. The interdependence of nature and man is crucial to our growth in every way and represents the perfection and harmony we seek to cultivate on our inside. But have you ever really stopped to immerse yourself in nature? Have you watched the miracle that is sunrise and sunset? Have you listened to the sound of water and observed its effect on everything around it; have you heard the sound of air? We are a part of nature as much as nature is a part of us.

Meditation

The practice of meditation, which produces a deep state of relaxation and quiets the babbling mind is considered a physical and spiritual wellness tool. Both the brain and the hormonal system (cortisol, the stress hormone) are affected. Mental clarity, stress reduction, mind-body balance, better sleep, and enhancing the effort toward spiritual awakening, are but a few of the benefits. To be still and allow the universe to bring to you what you asked for is much like the practice of meditation. The more I sat still and observed people's interactions and reactions, the more I understood about myself. This moment for me was magical. "Be still and know that I AM God," was playing out right in front of me. In my stillness, I began to recognize I was connected to Source and as long as I acted, Source would react with an equal and opposite reaction. Physics classes, biblical verses, and all those books in the vein of *As a Man Thinketh* now made sense.

For my meditation practice, I wake up most days between 3:30 and 4:00 a.m.. I used to set an alarm and now my body is used to it so I wake up without one. I chose this time to meditate because I am definitely not a night person and would fall asleep in the middle of my meditation. It is a wonderful way to start the day. Full of meditation and prayer, I especially love the way I feel, peaceful and energized.

Pleasure and Play

On my spiritual walk I came to appreciate play was something completely missing from my life and was an important part of pursuing joy. Play is a big part of who I am today even though what play looks like for me is very different from what most people find playful. Remembering who I was, the reason I am here, and what I am after, I am willing to use any tool in my toolbox to get there, especially one as enjoyable as play. This was a novel moment.

Rewards

The rewards of spiritual awakening are countless and priceless. You become better at everything, a better spouse, mother, leader, daughter, son, sibling, co-worker, etc. In an awakened state, there is a sense of inner peace, a sense of connectedness, a fine-tuned intuition, an understanding of synchronicity, compassion, the ability to let go, and the ability to extend true unconditional love to humanity. It is your best life as you have asked for it.

CHAPTER THIRTEEN
MANY PATHS

☥

BEFORE I END MY STORY, let me state, that there are as many paths to individual awakenings as there are individuals. Your path is the one that is right for you. Every soul has a different journey and there are situations and people on our path to guide us along. You might have heard the expression, "There is no chance meeting," or "When the student is ready the teacher will come." You may never fully understand the teacher-student relationship; how each of you impacts the other because, believe it or not, for them, you are a part of the puzzle of their lives.

There is no absolute about anything, as in there is only one way to your enlightenment or your spiritual walk. Your way is the way you take and is *the* way for you. Whether you walk, ride, fly, sail, or take the rail; whatever way you choose to begin your journey, you're sure to find your way. And it gets even more complex as there are paths within paths. Even within a mode of travel, we can take different routes. There are multiple roads and freeways, airports, and ports. Think of it this way, If you want to travel from LA to Long Beach, you can go by bus, drive, taxi, and tram, and each of those could take a different freeway or breezeway. Likewise, there are multiple ways to travel across continents, with multiple airlines leaving from multiple points headed to the same destination. In the future, because of the speed and advancement of technology, there could be even more modes of transportation to various destinations. "Beam Me Up Scottie," may become a reality! Just get there.

Because humans are complex, unique beings with vast cultural differences, the lens through which the world is interpreted will undoubtedly inform an individual's path. Although there may be many paths to a spiritual awakening, there are as we discussed earlier, commonalities as one journeys toward the same destination—remembrance. If your belief is anchored in religion as opposed to science, the message is the same. Return to everlasting life through the I AM.

My path emerged through my pain. I grew up in a religious tradition and rejected it because it did not have the answers I sought at the time, but later returned to find, now connected, it was my path that led me to many other spiritual, religious, and natural traditions. Additionally, I got to travel the world on my remembrance journey of returning to self. And here is the beautiful thing, the road continues for as long as you want or need it to. No matter what inspires you to be in remembrance of yourself, experiencing the freedom to be you again is perfection. On my journey, though my religious beliefs underlined my journey, I spent time studying different spiritual and religious texts for points of view. Through them, I experienced valuable teachings about spiritual awakening that have been enlightening, powerful, and beautiful. Someone else's path could have been triggered by the death of a loved one or the birth of a miraculous child; whatever it is, there is a loud vibration of a spirit in search of itself for one reason or the other.

AFTERWORD

I have risen above conditioned loyalty and erroneous stories. I have put down the burden of shame and reconciled morality. I have let go of the anger of hurtful conversations and grieved the loss of innocence.

I wanted to share the why and how of my journey. I was called to love and to stop the cycle of generational pain that shrouded my family and that could only be accomplished if I walked in my truth. It was through my focus on this that I felt the calling to do something big for the I AM. My story is my own and each member of my family has their version of what happened and it's all perfect. I hope that sharing my perspective helps people and like anything else, take from it what you need.

From my vantage point, to reach the pinnacle of "lasting success" one truly has to know thyself inside out to be able to make sound decisions that align with your values. But more than that, you become one with Source. I have put the word success in quotes because success for everyone is different. Regardless, to reach a place of true freedom in business or in our personal lives, one finds the key to loving oneself fully.

If seeking a life of fulfillment and joy is your aim, the why of the why is your desire to have your longing answered. To live in a state of joyful bliss is the result of seeing yourself in the full experience and expression of your own life. For me, this is a place where I find I can fully express the reason for my existence. I AM that I AM. I have fully claimed and am in communication with myself, others, and Source. That creates the oneness of the I AM. At the point of arriving at a Glorious Arising, there's a sense of awe, wonder, and curiosity. You are discovering the true essence and the miracle of who you are.

I believe the ultimate goal for us as human beings is to strip away the morass we gather along our life's journeys to find our way back to source. For my journey, love was what I sought. It's likely yours too because love is the language of the universe. Love is the least common denominator of all existence, and it is seeded within us. The ability to love, despite a challenging life, may be a difficult concept to hold onto when you are on your own, fighting for a place in the world with no safety net below you. But I truly believe, that "Love is All."

My awakening journey asked me to step away from the earthly meanings I'd placed on things and step into what I wanted to create. It asked me to suspend my earthly disbelief! This sounded farfetched but my guides asked me to imagine with them for a moment another possibility. Whatever your denomination, culture, sex, country, etc., you will agree there is something magical about the complex, interconnected, and interdependent world we live in. Simple questions such as, how does the world sustain oxygen at levels that never change? Why does the moon go to sleep when the sun rises? Why do we experience disease when the PH of our body shifts out of its narrow range? Why do animals and other living things obey the laws of nature instinctively? I believe it is because we all stem from the same source even though we are differentiated differently. We're simply a part of the process. No more no less.

If indeed the Divine Source is energy then we are all energy. The theory energy can neither be created nor destroyed then suggests, and it stands to reason, that the spirit within us and our soul, that which is divine, never dies after our physical bodies die. And consider this, what if for us to reconnect to Source we need to cycle through every life experience possible—love, anger, fear, confidence, joy, sadness, to return to its origin?

So, what if I told you not to worry because God has this? That you can let go and let God steer the wheel. You may say I don't believe in God. Great, you don't have to, however, this work is based on the understanding that there is something greater than us. Whether you believe in science, energy, God, Buddha, Allah, Jesus, or something else, there is something or someone keeping this world in its chaotic perfection.

In my perfect world, I AM truly free. The freedom I have stems from within. I live fully in acceptance of myself and everything around me, without expectations and I choose joy. I live as I have been created so I can be one with everything. The unity of all things is the answer we have been searching for, and especially in a world leaning more and more into the *Tree Of The Knowledge of Good and Evil*. When we have finally conquered our urge to follow the ways of the world that sprout from that Tree, what is left to explore is deeply rooted in the *Tree of Life*. But now our roots are connected to both trees: the *Tree of the Knowledge of Good and Evil* and *The Tree of Life*. Between them is our holy spirit. I used to ask what is between the two trees. Now I know in my being, that I AM that I AM. The Tree of eternal life, which is my soul, and the Tree of knowledge of good and evil, my body created in the garden of Eden, lead to my conscious which is the in-between the soul and the body. Once all operations, the many parts to a whole existence that is in you and me become one, we become like Christ. Looking at the two Trees from this vantage point we now will clearly see, they are one.

Again, some of what I have shared may not yet resonate with you but I encourage you to keep on your path, your way. What I have shared in this book are stories, processes, and tools that were helpful to me on my Glorious Arising journey. They could be beneficial to you too. Adapt them to your way or create new ways that can only be discovered by you. Our goals are the same—a return to innocence return to love.

So, this is me. Kiana Webb. I just told you about my journey. At the end of it all, I hope you will come away with thought-provoking questions, tools, and lessons to guide your journey back to the remembrance of self. I hope I helped you.

The last thing I want to leave with you is that YOU, and only you, are the key to your life. You truly are the I AM.

A Glorious Arising was the culmination of my walk with Faith, Hope, and Love. At the pinnacle of my career as the CEO of Webb Family Enterprises I was living with angst and a sense that there had to be more to life than this. My soul calling started making itself known. Two years before COVID-19 I shared with my family my need to move in a new direction. I had never been truly satisfied with the pursuit of just tangible success knowing a holistic approach to leadership was a key to our business success. It set in motion the wheels of change that arrived as a gift I would have preferred not to receive but embraced. That gift started me on a journey of self-discovery and my soul knew it was on its way home. The beauty of spiritually awakening is, as the Bible says, you have to share the Good News. Glorious Arising is my way of sharing and heralding my good fortune. Drawing on my years of leadership abilities and business acumen, I have created an environment for people to thrive, realize success on their terms, and design the life they desire—no matter their background or circumstances.

My book, documenting my journey, offers tools and resource-driven support for people who know something else exists for them and want to get to the next level of claiming their lives. Understanding you are the architect of your own life and that letting go of what no longer serves you will allow you to embrace a future that is completely and authentically yours. My lifelong pursuit of bringing people together for the greater good has informed my life even before my spiritual walk. Now armed with the shift in my paradigm, and empowered with spiritual grace, I am an even better vessel for others who wish to experience a Glorious Arising in their life.

I leave you with some questions to ponder

- Do you find yourself seeking your truth in others? In places other than yourself?
- Are you looking for a profound love? Are you looking for love from others to affirm you?
- Do you feel love for yourself?
- Are you willing to experience love by discovering all that you are and have created within yourself?
- Do you believe in the power of your love?
- Do you believe in love as a power that fuels life?
- Is there something that you want above all things? Something that will bring you the fulfillment for which you are searching? What does that show you about yourself?
- Are you looking to be seen by others? Can you see yourself?
- Is there something in the future that you want to feel successful about?
- Do you experience success in the small things, accomplishments, both or neither?
- Where do you look to see yourself as good? Is it someone else or something else?
- Do you set intentions for how you want to feel and see yourself?
- Are you hard on yourself?
- Do you want to be seen by others?
- Are you afraid or unwilling to look at all you are, see all that you are for yourself?
- Do you find yourself upset, annoyed, or frustrated by something someone else says or does?

- Are you willing to accept that these questions are opportunities for you to lean into the love that you are seeking? Are you willing to become the love that you are missing inside.

The benefit of A Glorious Arising is the fact that it's your glorious rising. It's your remembrance of self. The entire process of internal awakening is designed to help you love and respect yourself; to help you get to know yourself at your core; to help you feel good about who you are at all times; and to help you identify the things that are holding you back from the love that you are, have been and will always be. The ability to now see and recognize the control you've placed on yourself that others will ask you to let go...let go of all the loving ways you've learned to self-protect. Letting go creates the freedom to return to your first nature or the innocence of your youth. Being free to express love and embrace a glorious rising's path leads to the wisdom that brings us back to that place of no expectations, or judgments and to a place where we can truly experience the divine and the miracles of life. This is the place where you can begin to bask in the beauty of life. This is the place where you can attract all the things you've wished for, now able to claim the many gifts that will continually expand. The process of a Glorious Arising is not designed to harm people but rather to love, create, and be free to design the life we envision for ourselves.

A LOVE LETTER TO READERS

☥

Beloved,

That's my story. I am no longer suppressing it all. What can I say, other than, in trying so hard to hold it all together, it was no wonder it all fell apart. Crumbling like a golden tower. Nothing could have stopped it because I no longer had the strength to keep going as I had been. You may think the tower fell because of the incident with Kyle but the truth is, even before then, my foundation was crumbling. It was in rebuilding a firm foundation of love that I found the strength to conquer the illusions outside of me.

When the business sold, the two thoughts I had every morning that I am responsible for my parents' financial well-being, and Please God don't let me kill anyone today were over. That was a relief. I had done what I was supposed to and now it was my turn to create a future that was based solely on what I wanted. But without the support of my family in the way I'd expected and supported them all my life, I was crushed and scared that I would lose the very thing I'd spent a lifetime building, my family. But putting my family before God, and holding on to them hurt us all, especially me and that was not the answer. I see that now. Because of my indecisiveness, my fear became a stronghold that paralyzed all of us from moving on in a way that threatened the very financial future I worked so hard to build and when I thought I had let go, I soon came to realize that I had not fully.

It wasn't until I went on a ten-day writing intensive, that the final door was unlocked for me. This book has been healing. The thing that keeps us separated from all we are created to be is our need for control. I went from Faith, Hope, and Love to a Glorious Arisings—the place that is my realized soul, connected to the love that I AM, as myself, and others. Yet there is still more work to be done. If I could go, back the advice I would give myself and now offer to you is to let go, and simply surrender. The more you hold on to whatever or whoever wants to be free or keep you from your freedom is a sign of control. Let go of all the areas in your life that you are holding on to and turn toward the love that is in you; the love that you are. Release it all. Embrace the I AM with all your heart and put I AM first. Release the judgments, expectations, and conditions of what love is and rediscover all the love that you are. You are the key to your life. Only you can set yourself free. And like a bird free from its cage, take flight and soar. YOU GOT THIS!

I AM the way the truth and the life, no one gets to the father (God—which I believe is both feminine and masculine—except through me. Biblical text: John 14:6

Here I AM

I wish you well on your journey as new discoveries about yourself unfold and are revealed through Faith, Hope, Love, and Especially Love.

And Beloved. Thank you.

Glorious Arisings,
Kiana Webb
www.glorioussarisings.com

ACKNOWLEDGMENTS

I am forever grateful and humbled for the love of Jesus who said I AM the way the truth and the life no one gets to the Father except through me.- I Believe You, yes

I AM!

I would like to give a very special thanks to Anthony Liggins, who is truly a spiritual warrior, inspired artist, and the catalyst of this book

My children who have been a constant witness to my journey and with love never asked me to stop

My Love and soul sister Mercedes Marroquin, I would not have made it through the last twenty-four years without your friendship, love, and prayers

Anaya "Jennifer" Marroquin and Dalia Hamouda for keeping the business moving forward as I took the time to write and always supporting me as we healed and expanded our love together

For every person mentioned in this book, you are the teachers helping me grow my capacity to love

To Lisha Smith who was the first to say Kiana You and everything you create are Glorious Arisings

To everyone who has been with me on my journey, Thank You Thank You Thank you

www.ingramcontent.com/pod-product-compliance
Lightning Source LLC
Chambersburg PA
CBHW041105090726
47602CB00024B/175/J